'You'll ... ... ll l: < yc...
John's threa... were like a cuck...
there and pushed everything els...

Sam Wilkinson has become the latest target of John
Snow's bullying tactics. Even though there is no physical
violence, John's threats and insults have the power to
bring Sam's world crashing down around him. And
when nobody will listen, Sam decides the time has come
for him to take action. But Sam's attempt to stand up
for himself has consequences that could not have been
foreseen, especially by John . . .

ROGER J. GREEN was born in Buxton in Derbyshire in
1944. He taught for many years in Sheffield primary
schools and he lives in Sheffield with his family.

Cuckoos

Other books by Roger J. Green

Cuckoos

Roger J. Green

OXFORD
UNIVERSITY PRESS

OXFORD
UNIVERSITY PRESS

Great Clarendon Street, Oxford OX2 6DP

Oxford University Press is a department of the University of Oxford.
It furthers the University's objective of excellence in research, scholarship,
and education by publishing worldwide in

Oxford New York

Athens Auckland Bangkok Bogotá Buenos Aires Cape Town
Chennai Dar es Salaam Delhi Florence Hong Kong Istanbul Karachi
Kolkata Kuala Lumpur Madrid Melbourne Mexico City Mumbai
Nairobi Paris São Paulo Shanghai Singapore Taipei Tokyo Toronto Warsaw

and associated companies in Berlin Ibadan

Oxford is a registered trade mark of Oxford University Press
in the UK and in certain other countries

British Library Cataloguing in Publication Data available

ISBN 0 19 275144 1

1 3 5 7 9 10 8 6 4 2

Typeset by AFS Image Setters Ltd, Glasgow

Printed and bound in Great Britain by
Cox & Wyman Ltd, Reading, Berkshire

Pupils should be taught that there are life processes, including nutrition, movement, growth, and reproduction common to animals including humans . . .

Page 45, Key Stages One and Two of The National Curriculum

The result of Dante's experience in Hell was that he was again able to see the stars . . .

John D. Sinclair in his introduction to Dante's *Inferno* (Oxford University Press, 1939)

ONE

'Put everything down and line up quickly and sensibly for the video room. And quickly means now, not next Christmas, Adam.' Mrs Firth picked up the video from her table and surveyed wearily the line the class was making. She decided it would do and repeated her instructions to the straggling line.

Sam, who sat at a table by the door, had been having a bad afternoon drawing angles. The corners of the angles looked like melting ice cream cones with smudged blobs on their ends. Looking forlornly at the hopeless angles, not looking where he was going, Sam joined the work-shocked line of children. Sam's brain was confused with a tangle of angles and the confusion spread down his legs. He collided with John, also mathematically shocked, and somehow their legs and ankles locked together. John lost his balance and fell heavily against the wall, causing him to bang his elbow with a sound that matched the sudden pain.

John held the line up while he regained his balance, rubbed his elbow, and stared at Sam with accusation and fierce hatred. Caroline, who had been behind Sam in the line, did not dare move forward. She had the expression of someone who suddenly sees an unexploded mine in their pathway. She plucked at her lip nervously as John muttered threats to Sam, his mouth twisted with dangerous thoughts.

'You'll die for this, dickhead. I'll lock you up in my den for this.'

1

Sam and Caroline watched helplessly as John's mouth contorted as though some hidden electrical currents worked the muscles. Equally helplessly they watched the mouth and face return to normal and they watched John swagger away down the corridor to the video room. The children behind Sam and Caroline made no comment. They were used to John with his threats and tantrums and waited patiently like motorists pausing for a dangerous load to move on. When Sam and Caroline had recovered they followed John in thoughtful silence.

'Oh, for goodness' sake get a move on.' Mrs Firth's voice cawed irritably from the video room. 'Come along. Mrs Grey's class are due in here in half an hour. You lot are the doziest class I've taught in all my hundred years of teaching.' But the class made no response to the hopeful joke. They were all too busy watching where John would position himself in the room. They watched him with the attention they would have given to an escaped poisonous spider.

'Sam, could you hurry up, please? Why there has to be a two mile gap in every line this class makes I shall never understand.'

Sam moved forward in shock mode. Like everyone in the room he was deeply afraid of John. Sam was very much aware that John would carry out the threats he made. The great fear heightened Sam's senses. He sat down and saw with unreal clarity the varnished fingernail of the teacher tap the video controls with irritable precision. The nails made a soft rattle like seashells in a paper bag. Sam saw the golden bracelet the teacher wore, watched hopelessly the tiny golden horses fastened to it as they too, rattled the controls. 'I love horses,' Mrs Firth had told the class. 'Each of these little golden horses represents a childhood pony. I was young once upon a time.'

2

Sam, seated like the rest of the class on the floor, felt John's feet in his back. He felt himself being pushed along the floor, with great force, until he was shoved right to the front. Nobody liked to sit there. There was no carpet here and you had to sit with your head tilted back so that after five minutes your neck and back ached horribly. Sam felt John punch him into position with a final painful kick. Sam stared at the screen hoping John had finished now.

'Right, everybody. You *are* quiet this afternoon. I hope this does not mean you are all asleep. Well, you know that this half-term we are learning about how different kinds of creatures live. Sam, it would help you to learn if you watched my mouth as I speak. This video will tell us about the life cycle of cuckoos. It's enormously interesting and all ready to play.' She had left her reading glasses on the classroom table and her nails scratched lightly on the buttons as she squinted to find the PLAY button.

John took this opportunity to place his foot underneath Sam and shake it violently, so that the whole of Sam's body wobbled like a jelly on a plate. Several of the class laughed loudly. Sam said nothing. Experience told him that John could well leave him alone soon if he was lucky. And fear kept his mouth tightly shut.

'I do hope that silly laughter is not a sign someone is being silly,' said Mrs Firth, finally pressing a button she was certain said PLAY.

Sam watched in silent unhappiness as a blue sky flooded the screen. Miserably he became aware of a spring morning with a hawklike bird wheeling and circling high above the fields and woods. For a few seconds Sam envied the bird its freedom, wishing he was out in the fresh air and not imprisoned in this stuffy room with an ugly threat behind him. He watched the bird glide and float as it searched for the nest of its victim. The film was a well-made one and showed the cuckoo slowly sink earthwards to settle on a shaded branch where it could watch the nest it had chosen for its egg. The camera focused on the cuckoo's cold, determined eye as it watched the nest where its single egg would cause such devastation. It made Sam fidget. The cuckoo's eye reminded him of John's cruel eyes.

After unblinking watching the cuckoo suddenly and silently swooped down on a meadow pipit's nest. The mother meadow pipit had left her eggs to go and feed. The female cuckoo squatted over the nest and began to lay her egg with determined and shining eyes staring into the camera. Sam wanted to turn and look to see if John was watching him with eyes as unblinking and hard. He was sure he was.

The cuckoo drifted away and the meadow pipit returned unaware of the sinister developments. The camera speeded up and showed a blurred succession of days and nights to show that time was passing. Then the action slowed and focused on a May morning with rising sun catching the dew on bluebells and hawthorn blossom. The cuckoo's egg was about to hatch.

As soon as the cuckoo's egg tooth appeared through the shell Sam felt John's foot in his back. As the cuckoo pecked so John's foot kicked in matching rhythm in Sam's back. As the cuckoo chick finally hatched and the shell fell apart, John gave Sam a savage kick in the bottom of his back. Sam yelled out with pain and misery. Mrs Firth pressed the pause button and the triumphant cuckoo, tiny wings outstretched and glistening with egg, was suspended on the screen.

'What's the matter, Sam?'

'John keeps kicking me.'

'I'll move away, Mrs Firth,' said John smoothly. 'I was trying to get comfortable. It was an accident.' John stood up and moved away.

Mrs Firth beamed approval. The golden horses shook with satisfaction as she waved her arm to direct John to more space and comfort. She silently congratulated herself on how well she was managing John. She was having very little trouble with him. Nearly all the other teachers in the school saw him as a problem. Yet ever since he had joined her class a few weeks ago and had walked in with a litre bottle of expensive Spanish wine from his holidays, she had had no bother with him.

Some teachers said John was 'spoilt'. Mrs Firth suspected they were probably jealous, for John's parents were seemingly very rich. Mr Snow was a successful businessman and Mrs Snow was a barrister in a very expensive upmarket firm of barristers. There were teachers in the school who said John Snow 'was allowed to get away with murder' because his mother was a school governor and his father gave generous gifts of money to the school. One teacher said that John knew his mother was a clever lawyer and would get him out of any trouble he found himself in. Another said John was 'as thick as a short plank'.

Mrs Firth gave John a bright smile as she watched him settle down again. John had been known to lie down on a classroom floor and refuse to move if he could not get his own way. So far Mrs Firth had had no problems, no wobblies, no tantrums. She was sure she would cope. She was, after all, a very experienced teacher. And the other present John had brought her from Spain was delightful. It showed a view from John's father's villa in Spain. Mrs Firth had placed the picture in her hallway at home.

'I shall take him as I find him,' she had told the other teachers. 'I shall be firm but I shall avoid confrontations and negative criticisms.' She had said this drinking her raspberry-flavoured tea in the staffroom. 'He'll not roll around my classroom floor like a bad penny.' She had fished out the tea bag as she said this and dropped it in the bin with a plop for emphasis. She had smiled at the other teachers who hated and feared John Snow.

John was settled again. She gave him a final smile that she thought was firm, friendly, and all-knowing, then switched the video to play. The cuckoo, released from its static pose, wriggled about in the exquisite nest nudging the other delicate eggs. It made its naked wing stumps twitch and it twisted in the sunlight, attempting to dry mucus from its featherless body. Its eyes were still slits and this gave the cuckoo a cunning look. A fragment of shell stuck to the tiny hawkish beak.

Sam stared at the creature that looked like a miniature dinosaur from the forgotten past. Something in the appearance of the little monster made Sam suddenly turn to see what John was doing. He was watching him. Sam was aware that John had never taken his eyes away from his back. John's eyes were half closed, lizard eyes like the baby cuckoo.

Sam's brain catapulted into panic. He would have liked to have run from the room but he was hemmed in by children. Instead he fled into the secret places of his own mind where he stored facts about the thing he loved best, astronomy. In his spare time Sam tried to discover as much as he could about the universe, buy as many magazines as he could afford.

He began to wonder seriously if John was a type of alien species from beyond Earth. Sam knew John was different from all the other children in the class. He was unhuman-like in many ways. He rarely smiled, never cried, always seemed to have an expressionless reptile look like the small cuckoo. Perhaps, said an anxious voice in Sam's brain, John has been dumped here by some celestial cuckoos who wanted their baby to hatch on planet Earth. Perhaps John's real parents came from Mercury, that hot, vicious planet of fierce sunlight where nothing normal could live or feel. Perhaps that was why John was so unfeeling.

A snail shell tap of the OFF button reduced the screen cuckoo to a tiny dot at the centre of the screen. Mrs Firth faced the class. She was still pleased with herself and her tactics with John. She must be sure to tell Mike Johnson, the teacher who had taught John last year, about how well things were going. Mike had had nothing but trouble from John. He had accused John of being a bully, accused him of bullying the whole class. John had run out of school and fetched his mother and there had been terrible bother.

Mike used to enter the staffroom, his knuckles clenched, his breathing laboured, muttering, 'I'll do for that bloody kid before July.' He had tried to win John over by putting him in the football team but John could not cope with being on a side that might lose. He could not play unless he was the captain of the team. Yet here he is, thought Mrs Firth, sitting there on the carpet as good as gold. She would not be able to resist, as she sipped the blackberry tea she favoured for long staff meetings, telling Mike Johnson how well she was managing John.

'Stand. Now go back quietly and sensibly to the

classroom. And Sam and Jenny, I would like you to arrive before next week.'

Sam found he had to look to see what John was doing. It was as if his eyes were controlled by magnetic forces from far beyond him. He could feel his stomach swelling like a slowly blown-up balloon as panic slowly inflated inside him. John stared back with eyes as unfathomable as the cuckoo's. Sam could see the glint of a real gold chain round John's neck and vaguely wondered if it was an aerial receiving messages from his real parents on Mercury. He managed to stagger to his feet.

Mrs Firth bustled out of the room leading the line of children. She wanted to reach the classroom first so she could check the detailed planning notes she had had to make for the lesson. John followed her, seemingly obedient.

Sam was not fooled. He knew John, the infant space-cuckoo, interstellar pest and predator, sent from Mercury to torture Earthlings, would be waiting to get him in the shadows between the classroom and the video room. Between the rooms there was a recess with a noticeboard and a fire extinguisher fastened to the wall. Sam knew he would be there waiting to inflict another mean act as surely as the cuckoo in the film had laid its egg. He moved very slowly. He had never liked that bit of corridor and now he was certain that the fire extinguisher was a disguised small rocket designed for implanting eggs on unsuspecting parents on innocent planets. He moved out of the room. He was right. John was there, waiting in the half light between the rooms.

TWO

John waited by the dimly-glowing red fire extinguisher cone, still and disturbing as a stalagmite on a hostile planet. The other members of the class passed him warily, treading cautiously as though they were on a dangerous cliff path. Sam approached with fast-beating heart. The corridor was a dead end with the video room at the end. But John did not do anything as he passed. Instead he followed Sam closely, so that Sam could almost feel his breath down his neck, sticking close to him like an unwelcome shadow. Sam became aware of the heat from John's body, the heat he felt belonged to something that was not human.

As Sam put his foot on the step of the classroom door John placed the toe of his own shoe exactly on the heel of Sam's. At once Sam's trainer flipped off and Sam tripped over the dislodged trainer with his other foot. He fell into the classroom sprawling his full length on the carpet.

'Sorry, Sam,' said John loudly and confidently and Mrs Firth hardly glanced up from her curriculum notes. Then she removed her reading glasses and watched the class sit down. She began to explain to the class that they were going to make their own book about the cuckoo. It would be a small project that would last for a few weeks.

'It will be the first long unit of work that you have done for me. You will be able to show it to your parents on open evening and I will use it to assess you at the end of the year.' She handed out some thick card folders that looked pleasing and new and told them to design a cover for their project. 'I want a really good drawing on the front, using ideas you have just seen on the video. There are plenty of reference books, photographs, and photocopies round the room to help you. And I do hope, Sam, you are going to remove your shoe off the table. What? Yes, I can see the laces are knotted. Why you took it off in the first place, I can't imagine. You should be thinking about cuckoos, not footwear.'

She explained that she wanted careful lettering on the folder and that their names should be clearly printed too. She repeated all the instructions and the importance of the work. John put his hand up.

'Mrs Firth, can I go to the toilet?'

Mrs Firth almost frowned, a tiny ripple, like a small wave on a calm sea, passed over her forehead. She was irritated by the fact John wanted to leave the room at the beginning of very important work. On the other hand, she did not want trouble with him over an unimportant issue. That, in her opinion, was where the other teachers had failed.

'Do you really need to go, John?' She heard her voice, crisp, confident.

'Yes.' There was an unmistakable challenge in his voice.

To show that going to the lavatory was of no importance really, Mrs Firth picked up her reading glasses and looked at her mark sheet and gave John a dismissive bracelet-jangling wave that pointed to the door. Her reading glasses blurred the classroom and she did not see John give Sam a hefty nudge as he passed, making the pencil dig deeply into the thick paper. Sam had been absorbed with the idea of making letters to imitate the feathers of the cuckoos. Now the pencil had left a groove that would not rub out. John shut the door of the classroom loudly, not quite a rude slam, but loud enough to make everyone look up.

Light and sunshine suddenly appeared to fill the room. Sam decided he would cover the gash by drawing a stray fallen cuckoo feather, striped and shaded with his pencil. A robin perched on the rose bush outside the classroom and sang a couple of bars of its autumn song. The sun edged cautiously from behind clouds where it had been hiding and flooded the room with gold. A soft hum slowly grew from the children settling to work and relaxing. Caroline spread her fibre-tip pens out, secure in the knowledge that John was not around to meddle with them. Mrs Firth took a quick look at the staff meeting agenda and wondered if there would be time to get to Tesco's or Sainsbury's.

John sauntered very slowly down the corridor. He wanted desperately that his folder should be the best in the class, so he intended to make the toilet visit as long as he could. That way, on his return, he could have a good look round the class for the best ideas. Once he reached the toilets he remained still for a long, long time, hands in pockets, deep in thought. But his face showed no hint of what he was planning. Then he kicked open a lavatory door and walked in.

He kicked the door shut with more force than the first kick and saw some white flakes of paint spray off the door. John kicked the door again, fascinated by the tiny blizzard. He gave no thought to the damage. He thought the school was rubbish and the snowstorm of flaked paint proved it. He thought of the Men's Room at his father's business, its straw-coloured marble tiles, mahogany doors, shining brass, and taps that poured water on your hands at just the right temperature when you put your hands under them. And the cloakroom at his mother's firm had a tinkling fountain, lush ferns, a table with bottles of water on it and glasses, a fan blowing slightly perfumed air into the softly lit interior.

John stood up. He had no intention of flushing the old chipped lavatory bowl. He idly began to spin the toilet roll on its rusty wire holder, watching the white paper make pleasing loops on the floor. There was a suggestion, but only just, of a smile on his face. He enjoyed the television advert of the Labrador puppy and the toilet roll. He would have dearly loved a puppy of his own. But he heard his mother's calm, reasoning voice speak in his mind. 'No, John. Most things we can plan and arrange for you. But not a dog.' He did not wash his hands because the old sinks looked grubby, the liquid soap smelled of the low fat margarine his mother gave him, and the paper towels were rough.

In the classroom John saw the folders were well under way. Mrs Firth had asked for pictures that were 'scientifically correct'. John's lips curled in a sneer as he looked at cuckoos like sausages with legs as spindly as a single pencil line. The nests looked worse with pencil scribble imitating the careful construction of the pipits. They were all rubbish, thought John, greatly cheered by them. Except Sam's. Sam's lettering was neat. It looked like the hawkish feathers of the female cuckoo. Sam had made an excellent sketch of the baby cuckoo with egg on its beak. John made a swoop on Sam's gold ink fibre pen. Sam had been using it to show the rising sun glistening on the leaves and flowers round the pipit's nest.

'Can I borrow this? Thanks.'

Sam watched helplessly as the expensive pen, his best pen, was carried away. John knew what he would do now. He knew he could not draw as well as Sam but he would do something he thought he was good at. A deep silence fell upon the class. Mrs Firth surveyed them and thought how well she was coping with John. True, what he was doing did not appear to resemble a cuckoo, but he was interested and busy and she was sure it would have something to do with cuckoos. She decided not to ask. She recalled a supply teacher last year asking him what he was doing and then telling him what he was doing was incorrect. John had rolled under a table and sulked all morning. The year before that he had torn his work up and sprinkled it on Mrs Jackson's head after she had told him his work was not good enough. Mrs Firth had no intention of falling into that trap. She had thirty other children to teach.

Mrs Firth did not speak to John when he showed her his folder at the end of the afternoon. This time the reason for not saying anything was different. She was at a loss for words when she saw what John had done. John's cuckoo was a monstrous bloated creature, closely resembling Donald Duck, the only bird John felt he could draw properly. The giant bird was completely gold for John had carefully used up all of Sam's pen. John felt quantity in gold was the key to successful drawing.

The drawing had two bulging blue eyes that looked at Mrs Firth with defiant pathos. The disturbing blue of the eyes had been achieved by using most of Jenny's blue Day-Glo highlighter pen. Despite a smart real leather pencil case, designed to look like a marine's boot, crammed with expensive pens, John still preferred to use other children's. He had the superstitious belief that it was the pens people used that made them do good work.

The gross cuckoo straddled the folder and had a bubble emerging from its shining beak. Mrs Firth's bracelet shook very slightly as she put her reading glasses on and read, 'Hi, folks! I'm a real cool cuckoo chick, so watch out!' Now she had her spectacles on Mrs Firth could appreciate the full horror of the cover. She saw the chick had a truncheon tucked under a golden wing, very black, very shining, inked in with James's black metallic ink fibre-tip. Sara's white Tipp-Ex pen had been used to make contrasting white letters on the truncheon. Mrs Firth weakly read CUCKOO'S NITESTICK. She saw that the cuckoo wore a peaked cap in the design favoured by the New York cops. She saw the dreadful creation's legs were very sturdily drawn and sported motor-bike boots.

Oh, my stars, thought Mrs Firth as she feebly put the folder down. Whatever will his mother say when she sees that? She hoped and prayed John's parents were impressed by cartoon drawings. Some parents were but she suspected John's were not among their number. She nodded weakly. She said nothing. There was no point in a confrontation at the end of the day. She took control of herself and shouted loudly to the class.

'I want everybody to put their folders on my desk just like John has done. Sam? I did not give you permission to go. Please do not leave the room until I say so. Why you want to be the first to go I don't know. Pardon, Jack? No, I don't think rubbers are poisonous, it depends how much you ate.'

Irritation with the swollen cuckoo made her sound cross. She became silent again. John had pulled his folder out from the bottom of the pile and turned it round so she could appreciate the back. On the back cover, where she had planned the children could make a list of reference books they had used, John had drawn ten tiny cuckoos on motor bikes fleeing the giant cuckoo on the front.

Automatically, the children not seeing her amazement and horror, Mrs Firth clapped her hands. 'Right. You may all go now. I'll see you all tomorrow. Don't forget it's games in the afternoon and I shall be *very* strict with people who have forgotten their kit.'

She began to sift idly through the folders as the children left. She was tired and she was wondering about the best way to tell John his work was not appropriate. So absorbed was she with this problem that she hardly noticed Sam's folder with its observant drawing and stray cuckoo feather cleverly sketched near his name. How to manage John had pushed everything else from her mind.

Mrs Firth had prevented Sam's early escape from the classroom. He knew he must avoid John at all costs. His only hope now was to stay behind as long as possible and hope John would go home. With this plan in his mind he pretended to look for a lost felt-tip in his tray. Sam arranged his pencil crayons in their tin. John never wanted these. Like some thieving magpie, John seemed only attracted by bright and glittering pens. Then Sam jumped as the gold fibre-tip landed in his tray. He picked it up, guessing from the feel of it that it was quite empty. He shook it and as he had expected he could not hear the slosh of the gold ink any more. John had taken it all.

Sam became aware that John was staring at him, waiting for something. He trembled slightly as he walked over to the bin and dropped the useless pen into it. It made a clang as it hit the side of the bin. He would have liked to say, 'Thanks for using it all up, John,' but he did not dare.

15

'Thanks for lending me that pen, Sam,' said John loudly and pleasantly. 'There was just enough ink left in it for me to do my folder.'

Mrs Firth looked up from her table. Perhaps she was winning with John. He seemed anxious to be saying and doing the right thing. It will be a slow change, she thought to herself. A few steps each day. She decided not to say anything about the dreadful cuckoo. Perhaps she would think of a way round it when John was with his parents on open evening. They would have to realize John was not very intelligent. Perhaps the folder would be a way of saying that to them . . . She looked thoughtfully out of the window, struggling with the problem.

'Don't forget what I said earlier,' said John to Sam in a voice as soft as silk and quite beyond the range of Mrs Firth's troubled mind. 'Don't forget. Because I won't.'

'Goodnight, Mrs Firth,' said John, loudly now and brightly. 'Have a safe journey home. Take care.' John imitated exactly the phrases his parents used after a party as they said farewell to guests. Mrs Firth smiled and radiated pleasure as she said goodnight. Yes! She was winning with John.

Sam was left alone with Mrs Firth. He passed the time he needed for John to be well away by pretending he had a book stuck fast at the back of his tray drawer. He managed to pretend this for five minutes then he slipped out of the classroom. Mrs Firth was still looking out of the window, deep in thought. She did not notice him go or hear his soft, 'Goodnight, Mrs Firth.'

THREE

Sam looked down the corridor in the manner of an explorer surveying a new and dangerous land. Some minutes passed before Sam at last set out along the concrete floor. He felt wretched. It wasn't just the fact that John might be waiting. What also made him utterly miserable and alone was the discovery that Adam wasn't waiting either. Adam had been his best friend since they had started school together. But that, like everything else, seemed to be changing. Sam walked slowly and watched for John and thought of Adam.

On the first morning of the new class Mrs Firth had said she did not mind friends sitting together. She had two rules about that, she said. There must be two girls and two boys to every table and if friends stopped each other working they would be moved. Sam was still puzzled by that first morning. Adam and he had moved towards a nice new table by a bookcase with flowering plants on top of it. Then, oddly, Sam felt himself pushed and saw John sitting next to Adam. Sam, who had as little to do with John as he could, moved to a table by the door with its draught of cold air. He had expected Adam to follow. Looking back, he saw John next to Adam, emptying everything out of Adam's pencil case and examining his pens. Sam did not blame Adam for not leaving his pencil case with John. But from that moment Adam was no longer the friend he had been.

Cautiously Sam approached the cloakroom. He was uncertain when John would get him. It could be now, or

17

days away. One boy, last year, Thomas, had had to move school because John had made so many threats. Thomas, unable to explain his fear of John, had become ill. The doctor, half suspecting bullying, had suggested a change of school. The grown-ups were puzzled. The class were not. They knew how easily John escaped accusation. They also knew that John's threats were like a cuckoo's egg. Once laid, they stayed there and pushed everything else out of your life.

In the last few metres before the cloakroom door the sunlight made golden bars on the concrete as it shone through the windows. Sam found himself avoiding treading on the gold bars. It was a charm that might keep John away, at least for the next few minutes. The charm seemed to work for he found the cloakroom empty. A trainer lay in the middle of the large square space and Sam thought that in the old days Adam would have made jokes about someone having their leg cut off by a dinner lady. They would have no further use for the extra trainer and would just leave it in the cloakroom.

Sam stared at the lonely trainer and then at the pegs. They were quite empty. His coat was not there. There was no coat left by anybody else, no coats left on the floor waiting for the cleaners to put them on the pegs. The pegs themselves looked on, all-knowing and silent. Their round bulbous heads gleamed dimly. Not for the first time did Sam wonder if they were some kind of serpent, frozen into immobility by a distant space-lord, waiting for some coded command to come alive and take over the school and the world. Then he faced the truth. John had taken his coat when he had asked to go to the toilet. This was the beginning of John's programme of torture.

The fact that John had meddled with his property worried him more than the actual loss of the jacket. There would be a row at home, of course, for he had not wanted the jacket in the first place. It had come from Marks & Spencer's and he had wanted one from the Adidas shop. His mother would say he had lost it on purpose and there would be a boring lecture on what the family could and could not afford. But he could deal with his mother. He could not deal with John waiting to get him and taking his things.

Inside he felt as empty and desolate as the school around him was, now that everyone had gone home. He knew he would have to go through all the procedure of saying his coat was missing. He knew the truthful statement 'John has taken my coat' would be useless. 'Oh, Sam, you mustn't say such things . . . Sam, you must not accuse people if you have no proof . . . Oh, Sam, what a terrible thing to say . . . Someone has taken yours by mistake . . . ' He heard all the grown-up voices in his mind. He knew he must go through the useless ritual of saying his coat had gone. It was a ritual as pointless as clearing your bedroom, thought Sam, as he waited outside the headteacher's room. Mrs Highfield was the headteacher and he would begin with her. He knew Mrs Firth was in the staffroom or had gone home. He had heard her slow steps in the corridor as he looked in the cloakroom.

Ten minutes later he was in front of Mrs Highfield who was breathless from selling the school. 'Selling the school' were her words for the talks she gave to parents who were thinking of sending their children to her school. Mrs Highfield was a large woman who favoured tentlike structures for dresses, the tents pegged down with many gold ornaments. Her room bristled with files and booklets about what the school was doing. She had a booklet for everything parents and inspectors might want to know about. Graphs, computer printouts, charts of the school's money supply, were pinned neatly to boards around the room. One clip frame displayed a child's painting. She loomed and rustled over Sam as he told her what was missing.

'Sam, dear . . . couldn't it have waited? It'll probably be brought back tomorrow by somebody who has taken it by mistake . . . Now, dear, go and find a coat in lost property and borrow that until tomorrow, please. Explain to your mum and dad there has been a misunderstanding.' She switched on a big smile for Sam that vanished as she reached for, and picked up, a huge red file labelled SCHOOL FINANCE.

'What did you say, Sam? There wasn't a spare one left in the cloakroom? Are you sure? Oh dear, Sam, I've a staff meeting. I should have been there five minutes ago. It's all about the inspectors' coming visit and our money.' The smile was turned on again like a seaside illumination. 'Could you possibly find Mrs Davidson, the CCA in the reception class. She will be there until four. She will help you.'

Sam stood aside as though he was on the kerb of a busy street. Mrs Highfield, swaying with papers and files, tottered past him. He heard her sigh. A flicker of concern stirred in her mind for Sam, through the first delicate velvet blows of a coming headache. In the old days she would have had time to put her arm round Sam with his pale strained face. Long experience had told her when a child said one thing it usually meant something else as well. But these days she felt as if she was swimming in a huge swimming pool of paper and getting nowhere.

She had had a hell of a day. A leak had spouted in the ceiling of a cloakroom, a boy had thrown a stone at a passing bus at dinnertime and his mother had said it was the school's fault. She said if the school had had a bigger fence the stone would not have gone over and hit the bus. Then Mrs Turner had gone home leaving Class Two to be taught. Mrs Turner had said she had food poisoning and said she had caught it from the cut price meat in the school dinner she had eaten. Mrs Highfield staggered up the stairs and for a brief moment wondered if the lost jacket was someone bullying Sam. She felt her head pounding as she reached the top of the stairs that led to the staffroom. Well, at least bullying had been dealt with, she thought. She had arranged parents' meetings and school activities all last term and had a glossy booklet to show for it. She wished the problem of finding more money for books could be solved as easily. Sam forgotten, she put her shoulder to the door and was greeted with the aroma of instant coffee and blackberry tea bags.

Sam found Mrs Davidson washing up paint pots in the reception class. She was wearing a pair of bright yellow rubber gloves that dripped soap froth as she turned to smile at Sam.

'Are you quite sure you brought a coat to school, Sam? It was a lovely September morning this morning. You're sure?'

'Yes,' said Sam almost snappishly. Of course he was sure, as sure as he was that John had something to do with the loss of it. He was becoming miserable. He was frightened of John waiting to get him outside. He had realized the lost coat would mean no pocket money until another had been saved for.

Obediently he followed Mrs Davidson on the useless

21

lost coat trail: the dinner room, the benches in the nature area, the hall, the library, the cloakroom (Just in case you missed it—as if he had), and finally to the cleaners. They were struggling with a Hoover the size of a small dinosaur. They were glad to pause and rest.

'I meant to go back and pick it up but I started to help Liz lug this great thing to the library. It's stuffed behind a toilet in the boys', if that's the one.'

Mrs Davidson moved purposefully towards the toilets, Sam following imagining all that John might do next. And there the coat was, in the third one along, stuffed in a tight ball behind a dusty pipe. There were some flakes of paint on the floor and Mrs Davidson gave a small cluck, like a curious hen, as she stirred the fragments with her shoe. Then she retrieved the coat, zebra-striped with dust and its collar wet with slime.

'Somebody's put wee or spit on my collar,' shouted Sam, desperate to seek help.

But he was careful not to mention John. He knew if he did John would double his torments. And Mrs Davidson would bleat about it every time she saw John. 'I hope you haven't been messing with coats in the toilets, John,' and John would glower and make Sam's life even worse. That was the way things worked.

Mrs Davidson almost snatched the coat back off Sam. She took the coat to the sink and pulled violently at some green paper towels and began to wipe the collar. It did smell peculiar, she thought, but she had no intention of saying that to Sam. It was likely to be something off the floor. Now that money was short there was no longer an army of cleaners in the school every night. The toilets were not as sparklingly clean as they used to be.

She returned the jacket to Sam who was looking at her accusingly. His face was white, his eyes wild, his whole appearance was aggressive. Mrs Davidson wondered, not for the first time, what life did to children. Personally she blamed the television and all the violent films. She could remember Sam when he first came to school aged four, a bright, happy little boy. They had had an infant disco that year, she recalled, and Sam had announced that he was her boyfriend and had danced with her all disco long. That bright little four year old was now a sullen, cheeky, and sour-faced eleven year old.

'It's all right now. Whatever it was has gone now.' She smiled, trying to thaw Sam's wintry glare.

'It hasn't. Somebody's done that on purpose.' But the disguised cry for help was misunderstood.

'If that's what you think, Sam, find Mrs Firth or Mrs Highfield and complain to them and not to me. They're in a staff meeting. It's an important one. They won't be pleased to see you worrying over something that's been sorted out.' Her pride was hurt. She had found the jacket after all.

'I will find them, don't worry,' shouted Sam, unhappiness making him sound rude. Minutes ago he was for keeping everything quiet. But shouting had given him a surge of temper and confidence. And he could not stand the weeks of John's daily attacks. And telling someone delayed the time of leaving school. The fear of John waiting for him and dragging him away made him tremble and feel sick.

FOUR

Mrs Firth climbed the stairs thoughtfully and deliberately to the staffroom. She was tired after a long day's teaching but determined not to show it. She found she was the first to arrive in the staffroom, and she plugged in the kettle. It quickly boiled and snapped off with a bang that made her jump and the gold ponies shudder. She looked on the draining board for her beaker, a large white one with a glowing smiley face on it. She rummaged in her bag and found the essential blackberry tea bag. She made her tea in the beaker then collapsed on a chair with a sound like a balloon emptying itself of air. She watched the other teachers come in from behind a barrier of blackberry steam. She turned eventually to Mrs Stone who came to sit next to her.

'I'm absolutely knackered. It feels light years since the holiday.'

Mrs Stone sipped her own Nescafé. 'How are you coping with the Monster?' Mrs Stone followed the adventures of John with some anxiety. She knew if Mrs Firth became ill the head would ask her to look after John in her class. John demolished supply teachers with the efficiency of a bulldozer, leaving them quivering wrecks of despair.

'He's no trouble, really,' said Mrs Firth very loudly. She liked to boast of her thirty years of teaching and how well she could manage children. 'He actually said "sorry" to Sam Wilkinson this afternoon. Then he moved himself away from something that could have triggered a tantrum. A little bird tells me I'm not going to have the trouble that some have had.' She gave a triumphant look through the scented steam in the direction of Mike Johnson who had taught John the year before, or tried to. 'You see, I don't confront him. I don't collide with him. I encourage him. I can't have him disrupting the class with all we're supposed to teach in Year Six.'

'Has his work improved?' asked another teacher. 'It was beyond the pale when I had him. And his lovely mother and father always blamed me. Of course, I wasn't allowed to say anything.' She looked round to make sure the headteacher had not yet arrived. 'We mustn't upset his parents. All the money and help they give to the school might stop and she might give up being a governor.'

'His work is dreadful,' conceded Mrs Firth. 'I asked him to draw a cuckoo chick this afternoon and he drew bloody Donald Duck dressed up as a New York cop.' The room rippled into nervous laughter. The teachers found the Monster, as they called him privately, a worrying but fascinating topic.

'That's all he's got in his head,' said Mike Johnson. 'Between going for his no-expense-spared session in the gym with Daddy and swimming with rich Mummy darling, he's plonked in front of the box with an endless supply of videos. He's to be pitied really. He's got everything money can buy, yet he's as empty of experience as a comic book. On top of that he's not very intelligent—'

'The rest of the class are sweet and delightful,' said Mrs Firth sensing she was no longer the centre of the conversation. 'I think he'll do well this year.'

'That class are sweet and delightful because they're scared out of their wits by that muscle-bound empty-headed hulk. I'd bet a grand, if I had it, he's made someone's life a misery in your classroom today. That's how he gets his kicks. He's—'

'Are you telling me, Mike, that I do not know what is going on in my own classroom?' She scowled at the other teacher over the round smiling face painted on her beaker.

'Your tea bag smells absolutely delicious, dear,' said Mrs Stone loudly. As deputy head of the school she was well aware of the savage rows that could develop at the end of a long day. When teachers fell out it was so much harder to sort them out than the children.

'He is a problem though,' said Mr Brown who taught an infant class. 'We daren't tell his parents the real truth in case they take him away. We've no time to really help him sort things out—'

'Could we begin, please?' said Mrs Highfield. She had staggered in, made a coffee, popped three aspirins in her mouth with her back to the teachers and now, arranging her folds and files, she was ready to begin. 'We have a lot to discuss that is very important. Firstly I have the date of the inspectors' visit. Then I want to see if we can spend what little money we have on the books we really need. So let's forget John and make a start.'

Sam climbed the stairs to the staffroom, placing both feet side by side on each step. He had climbed stairs like this when he had been a little boy. He suddenly wished he was back in the infants. The days then seemed rosy and lit with a golden light. Some days his mother had come and helped in the classroom and after school they had gone to the shops together. Now he felt on his own, isolated from everybody. In those days Adam and he had always been in charge of the computer. They had always been able to get it going when the screen went blank or it bleeped like a wounded alien.

Half-way up the stairs he stopped. He looked at the jacket over his arm and thought he would never wear it again. He could not bear the thought of it near his skin or neck. He decided if his mother made him wear it he would wear a football scarf round his neck. He knew John did not support City as he did, but a cousin had left a scarf like the one John wore. He would wear that. He did not want to give John any opportunity to make remarks about anything. He went up another step. He counted eleven bottles of children's milk outside the staffroom door and wondered vaguely if the teachers had a bottle of milk with a straw after a meeting. Then he suddenly climbed the rest of the stairs in the normal way and knocked.

'The inspectors will want to look at everything,' he heard Mrs Highfield say in her loud assembly voice. 'They will look around your classroom, look at your planning, the books you are using, the children's work, displays, how the room is organized, how equipment is set out—'

'Will they want to see the colour of my underpants?' Sam heard Mr Johnson ask in an innocent way. In the endless laughter and uproar that followed Sam's knocking went unheeded. The noise became so loud that Sam was quite disgusted with them. The teachers were making more noise than the class did on a wet dinnertime, when rain poured and the dinner ladies shouted. He gave the door a kick but nothing happened. He gave up and slowly returned down the stairs. Maybe it was safe. Perhaps John would have gone home.

Outside in the street the world looked grey, sad, Sam thought, as soon as he saw it. Usually the school entrance was a cheerful place with children and parents coming and going. Above, heavy mud-coloured clouds had seeped round the gold of the sun. Sam felt a drop of cold rain on his cheek as he turned to look in every direction for a waiting John. A crisp packet blown by the wind made a surprisingly loud rattle and Sam jumped. Rain began to whisper, patter, then rattle in the big holly bush by the school gate. Sam sighed. He would not wear his jacket. The thought of the wet on the collar made him feel sick.

He thought he saw a shape vanish into the overgrown hedge of number nineteen which was on the road leading home. The hedge was never cut and had made a tunnel as it reached out to the cherry tree on the roadside grass verge. No way, thought Sam, no way am I going to pass that hedge and overgrown garden. He turned to look in the other direction and tensed as he looked at the entrance to the narrow lane that led from the road there. That lane followed the back of gardens and was narrow, dank, and lonely. It led to the common where he suspected John might have his den.

Not that he was sure about the den. There had always been rumours in the class that John had an exclusive den. Some said it was under the big double garage of John's house, equipped with a web site, games, billiard table (full size), bed, hi-fi, satellite television, and a jacuzzi. Others insisted it was in the loft of the big house

John lived in. A few were convinced it was in a tree house that you could just make out from the road. But the majority view was that it was on the common near the empty block of flats.

These flats were the local meeting place of a teenage gang. Jack Matthews had told the class that John had bought his way into the gang and gave them money for cigarettes and lager. Sam found that perfectly believable. He had seen the gang when he had been walking the dog and he had seen they had plenty of cigarettes and cans. Sam shivered a little. Like the rest of the class he was a little scared of these teenagers. The thought of John combining with them added a new dimension to his growing fears.

Neither way was safe. He decided he would catch the bus and return home from a quite different direction. It was a very long way round but he was certain John did not know that way. He reasoned that if John was watching for him he would see him getting on the bus and think he was going into town, meeting someone or swimming. Sam made a dash across the road and felt the rush of cold air on his wet shoulders. It was a school rule never to cross this section of road, but the lollipop lady had long since vanished. And Sam was not interested in rules at that moment.

At the bus stop he waited and waited. The rain, now thoroughly organized, became a downpour that soaked Sam to his skin. The jacket stayed over his arm. All the time his head turned in the rain, first to look at the dark, dripping, overgrown garden, then to the shadowed entrance to the shady lane to the common. The colour of Sam's T-shirt changed from white to a translucent grey like winter sleet.

The rain chilled his body and spread a misery into his mind. For a time he stopped thinking about John (although his head still turned) and thought about something that lived in the land of his mind like a dragon in a fairy tale. When he had been a few days old he had been left, abandoned on the steps of a side entrance to a local hospital. He had been securely and warmly wrapped in a blanket in a large cardboard box and someone later said they had seen a young man and a woman running away. They had never been traced.

Sam had been found by a policeman, PC Samuels, who had taken a great interest in the abandoned baby. He still sent Sam handsome gifts at Christmas and the guessed date of his birthday. The hospital named Sam after the policeman. Shortly afterwards the couple, the couple he now called Mum and Dad, fostered him, then adopted him.

On good days, this story, big as a dragon, seemed to be a wonderful story with a happy ending and the dragon basked peacefully and let Sam get on with his life. But on bad days, like this, the dragon filled his mind with bitter smoke and fog. On those days he wondered why he had been abandoned, why he had been rejected and sometimes he could not think of anything else. On those days the dragon belched out a banner from its mouth with the words 'Why did it have to happen to me' written on it with words of fire.

They abandoned me, left me, he thought, slumped and dejected, holding out his hand to stop the approaching splashing bus. I was left, just like that cuckoo left its egg this afternoon. I'm just a human cuckoo, he thought as he boarded the bus.

In the bus rain trickled down off him and made a neat pool at his feet. As the bus passed Adam's house he saw Adam in the front room, bent over a screen, saw the glow of a fire. The dragon cast a total shadow of sorrow and self pity in Sam's brain. He had taken fifty pence to school that day with the idea of spending it on crisps for himself and Adam after school. Before today he had thought Adam was still his friend. Now he knew Adam was gone for ever. Now he had to spend his precious pocket money escaping John. With his mind clouded with these dark thoughts, Sam left the bus at Rowan Avenue, well over a mile away from his house. He walked across a little park that was the territory of other children from other schools. Unhappy as he was he felt comparatively safe as he made his way home through streets unknown to John.

The woman whom Sam now called 'Mum' without a second thought, was in the kitchen when she saw Sam trudging up the path. She had just kicked her shoes across the kitchen. She had been on her feet all day at the shop where she worked. One of her toes throbbed and stung with a vicious corn and she was angry she had forgotten the corn plasters from Boots. She felt worn out for she had left the house at eight that morning. She stared at Sam in disbelief as he squelched his way to the door with his coat over his arm. Her nagging corn made her temper flare up, like petrol poured on a fire.

'I was just getting worried about you. Where've you been? Adam's? You weren't here when I phoned at four. And now just look at you. You're wet through. And if you think by refusing to wear that coat I'll get you one from that other shop you can think again. You don't help things you know, when you behave like this. It's not fair on me. You'd better get in a hot shower, put that vest in the washer, and hang that coat near the boiler, that coat that cost all of forty pounds, in case you've forgotten. Go on, get up the stairs. I don't want to talk to you when you behave like this. Go on. I've enough to do without seeing to drowned rats.'

Sam turned forlornly away towards the stairs. As he passed the phone it began to ring and Sam snatched at it, desperately hoping it was Adam suggesting something to do after tea. At first Sam could hear nothing, so he spoke his own number into the phone. Still Sam could hear no voice, only a sound that sounded like breathing and a distant radio or television. Then, soft, very sinister, came the voice of John. Sam had not imagined John to be capable of such quietly spoken words.

'I've not forgotten.' Then Sam heard the click of the receiver and the purr of the dialling tone. Sam let his own receiver fall back with a crash.

'Who was that, Sam?'

'Nobody.'

'It must have been somebody.' Mrs Wilkinson stopped rubbing her corn against her other leg and came into the hall. 'There must have been someone. Mrs Grey was saying at work burglars are ringing up to see if the house is empty. Who was it?'

'I don't know, do I? How should I know?' Sam made for the stairs.

'Watch that tongue, young man. Now what do you want with your pizza? Sweetcorn? Jacket potato? Beans? Oven chips?'

'I don't mind.'

'Whatever's the matter with you, Sam? I've had a terrible day in the shop and the last thing I want is one of your moods. Is there anything wrong? Tell me . . . Well, get in the shower, because I warn you, I can't take much more today.'

Sam climbed the stairs and closed the bathroom door with a bang. His mother, hearing the bang, sighed, then thought to herself Sam was growing up. Next year at this time he would be at the comprehensive school. Sam's brother had been just the same when he was eleven. Too busy to be bothered with the family any more, thinking only of his friends and school and wanting her to mind her own business. She gave a long sigh. She loved Sam and her own boys, but some days she felt utterly worn out with them all. Feeding them and clothing them seemed to push everything else out of her life. She returned to the kitchen. Sam would have salad and like it.

Sam sat on the chair in the bathroom staring straight ahead. It would have been better if John had told him exactly when he would get him. Then he could have hidden, pretended to be ill, not go to school that day . . .

'Tea's ready,' came his mother's voice. Sam had not even been in the shower. He had been thinking of all the things he knew John could do for fifteen minutes.

FIVE

John made his way noiselessly, catlike, across the
lounge of his house and out into the hall. This was easy,
his slippered feet made no sound on the deep pile of
the carnation-coloured carpet. He stood by the highly
polished hall table where three machines lay obediently
side by side. There was the fancy black and ivory phone,
inlaid with brass, a restored model of the 1920s. Next
to it was a state-of-the-art fax and a sober black
answering machine. John looked over his shoulder to
see that he was not being observed and then slid the local
directory from its shelf. Using a finger to point, breathing
heavily, looking over his shoulder now and again, John
took some time to find what he wanted. He had always
found the alphabet a mystery. Looking yet again over his
shoulder he dialled Sam's number. He picked up the
receiver from the mirror-like surface of the table, turned
to face the kitchen, spoke softly into the mouthpiece. On
no account must he let his mother hear of his plans for
Sam Wilkinson.

After the first sentence John saw a shadowy blur of a
figure on the glass of the hall door. John at once put the
phone down and hurried to the front door. A free
newspaper, delivered to all the houses, was beginning to
wriggle through the solid brass jaws of the letterbox. It
was a struggle, for the letterbox of the Snows' had a
vicious bite. John rapidly keyed in a number on a panel
by the door and the front door swung open with smooth
precision. The teenager delivering the paper looked
astonished, then grinned.

'Cheers, mate!'

'OK,' replied John. He felt a glow of satisfaction from the older boy's smile. He wanted the friendship of the teenagers in the district. He kept the door open as he watched the boy walk down the brick paved drive, past the huge tubs crammed with garden-centre flowers, past his mother's big new car parked outside the double garage. John saw the boy stop to admire the car. John himself took in the details of the teenager, his jacket, his boots, his haircut.

The teenager closed the big hardwood gate and went over to a friend waiting astride a small motorbike. He hoisted his rucksack of papers over his shoulder and got on the bike. He said something to his friend and they looked towards John and smiled. Then they vanished in a haze of blue exhaust. The final smile gave John great satisfaction. He knew they were part of the gang that messed about on the common. They were part of a fantasy plan he had for capturing Sam Wilkinson. John watched the road for some time, deep in thought, then closed the front door with a louder bang than he had intended.

'What was that, John?' A brisk precise voice spoke from the huge dining kitchen at the end of the hall, a room shimmering with spotlights and whitewood fittings. 'I said what was that noise, darling?'

'I was just collecting the free paper for you.' John adopted the same smooth voice that he used for Mrs Firth at school.

'Thank you, darling.' She said nothing else. She was a barrister and did not believe in using words that were not strictly required.

John returned to the lounge almost smiling. He was sorry that he had not told Sam Wilkinson exactly what his plans were for him, but he had let him know he had not forgotten.

John made his way to one of the three long settees where he had made a nest. The nest consisted of seven cushions and he climbed into it, elbowing the cushions until they were comfortable. Once the contours were moulded round his own large body he reached out for a can of Coke from the nearest coffee table. He balanced the can on a cushion so he could drink it when thirst overcame him.

He reached out for a small bag of low-fat crisps (his mother strictly rationed crisps) and balanced them on another cushion. One crisp fell from the packet and at once a small grease stain spread on the rose-coloured velvet of the nest cushion. Glancing in the direction of the kitchen John promptly turned the cushion over and replaced the crisps.

Before he made the phone call John had been drawing. He had a large pad of expensive A3 cartridge paper, vastly superior to the paper available in school. The floor was littered with screwed up sheets John had attempted. He had been trying to draw a scientific picture of a cuckoo like Sam Wilkinson's. The screwed up balls of paper concealed pathetic jumbles of pencil lines. Failure had angered John and steered him to the telephone. Now the sketch pad blossomed with Donald Duck and the Simpson family. The head only of Superman was tucked into the corner of the page.

John tossed the pad from his nest and heaved and lurched, searching for the hand control for the cinema screen television and video in the corner of the lounge. He discovered he was sitting on it. During the earthquake the can of Coke had tilted and spilled a frothy serpent that crawled over two other cushions. John swore fluently under his breath. He turned the cushions over, hoping Mrs Douglas, the cleaning woman, would do something with them tomorrow. Then he aimed the hand control at the screen.

Pictures from the video tape shimmered to life on the screen. John watched with birdlike intensity the adventures of a New York street gang. The leader of this trigger-happy gang fascinated John enormously. John's lips curled, threatening a smile, exhibiting more movement than they had made all day, except when he had curled them at the school dinner custard. Twice John put the picture on hold, twice he rewound the tape as if he wished to remember how the gang leader behaved.

After the gang leader was arrested (concluding a very bloody and noisy car chase) John watched three times the man being locked away in the cells. John appeared to be memorizing something for his own purposes. He was as alert as if he was learning a lesson. He missed nothing. During the court case the gang leader shouted abuse at the woman judge and John leaned forward in his nest. The can of Coke imitated the angle of tilt and oozed another quiet brown snake, but this time John was unaware of the spillage. He leaned back as he watched the gang leader create another gang within his prison walls. The whole film seemed to be of great significance to him. He had indexed the tape so he could rerun it back to the taking of the gang leader to prison and the shouting of foul abuse to the woman judge.

Finally, after several reruns of favourite sections he let the credits roll and the music play. He relaxed on the cushions, eyes half closed like a bird of prey after a big meal. This ecstatic trance was shattered by his mother's voice. She had heard the film ending.

'Time to eat, John.'

Mrs Snow prided herself on running a career and family in perfect harmony. She boasted of it in fact. She was a very successful barrister and her clients perfectly understood she was not available on certain days. She was so efficient they were prepared to wait. When she was in court arrangements were made for John. Her husband and she took John out four nights a week to martial arts, a gym, swimming, and the shopping mall. Tonight was John's video night and the night his mother did her homework, as she called it, spreading the kitchen surfaces with documents and printouts. The computers flickered, the lights glared and John came into the kitchen. Mrs Snow controlled everything she came in contact with.

'Now, my chick.' Mrs Snow's grandmother had called her that when Mrs Snow was young. Mrs Snow continued to use it. She felt it had a homely old-fashioned touch.

John slouched into the kitchen under the keen bright stare of his mother. She was still wearing her business suit with its sharp-cut shoulders and her diamond earrings glittered in the kitchen lights.

'Now, chicken. There is pasta, there is chicken, there are pizzas, there is crab with avocado, bread, salad, low fat sausage, some virtually fat free burgers, some turkey roll . . . the choice is yours, my chick.'

It was strange that when John's mother gave him such a wide choice it did not feel like a choice. John slumped under the brilliant smile which diminished a fraction as he remained silent, underwhelmed by the list of food. Mrs Snow gave a sideways glance at a laptop screen to see that it was still retaining the case notes as she had instructed it. The smile waned a fraction further. She whisked a stray length of pink legal tape that had escaped from an old will. It dangled from her long fingers like a captured worm. The bright smile had almost gone.

'Hurry up, darling.' The change from a chick to a darling warned John that proceedings were not going satisfactorily.

'I'll have some crab and salad and bread.' The gaze hardened. 'Please.' The smile returned. 'Can I make a sandwich and watch my video again? My favourite bits?'

'You know I like us to eat together and frown upon grazing in the lounge. But for once, my chick, you may. I have a big case tomorrow and I would like to concentrate. If you are making a sandwich you will find some half fat butter spread in the small fridge.'

At nine o'clock precisely, John left his nest and switched off the video. He threw away his failed art and savagely squeezed the empty diet Coke can before dropping it into the hand-painted Japanese waste-paper basket. John went to the door of the kitchen. His mother was absorbed with some photocopies. A bottle of wine had appeared. This was the night when his father worked late too. Later Mr Snow would appear with a takeaway and the wine would flow and John's parents would discuss the triumphs of the day. John stayed in the doorway for some time, a dark outline gazing at the brilliance of the kitchen.

'Goodnight, Mum. I hope you win.'

'Oh, I shall win, my chick. Goodnight.'

John cleaned his teeth with passion. Dentists impressed him. The ones his mother selected for him always had big fast cars and solid gold watches. He liked the adverts where there was a battle in the mouth between the bacteria and the toothpaste. It gave John pleasure to end the day winning one certain victory. He paused as he crossed the bedroom and stared at the view across the garden trees towards the smaller houses. He caught a glimpse of Sam's middle brother cycling furiously home. John wished he had brothers, lots and lots of them. Sometimes he felt so lonely that it hurt. He turned back to his bedroom where no expense had been spared. Another television, hi-fi, a brand new computer. He ignored all these and got undressed and climbed into bed.

He began to construct another nest around himself, a nest he built every night. It consisted of model soldiers, furry animals, and a great number of blank-faced teddies, the kind bought from card and gift shops. Two battered stuffed dogs were pulled to either side of him. Without this barrier to loneliness and other feelings hard to explain, John found it difficult to sleep. The toys kept the shadows from the garden from coming in and provided uncritical company.

He lay still for some time, breathing heavily, then he began making small adjustments to the circle of toys. Then he dimmed his bedside lamp and as his eyes accustomed themselves to the dark he lay and stared in the direction of Sam Wilkinson's house. He could see the house, quite clearly, over the low shrubbery beyond the long lawn. John's house was almost on top of the hill and Sam's house was half-way down it. Although John's mother had planted numerous exotic trees and evergreens you could still see the other houses. John lay and stared at Sam's house for a long, long time.

The intense stare at last began to waver and John drifted into a light sleep. This was shattered by the slam of a heavy car door, a blaze of security lights, and purrings of automatic doors. John's father had arrived home. He liked to make his presence felt and had once told John that was what life was all about. John heard some talk between his parents, heard his father come upstairs and make for his parents' bathroom. He heard the thunder of distant taps filling the bath, heard faint splashing, heard the faintest tap of Harrods' gold-topped bottles containing colognes and aftershaves being replaced on the marble washstand.

John heard the swish and rustle of his father's silk dressing gown as he came on to the landing and he could smell the expensive musky fragrance of his father. He steeled himself for the scheduled late night visit, a visit paid every late working evening. He was saved by the trill of a phone in his father's dressing gown pocket. Rich fragrance and his father's determined voice drifted into the twilight of John's room. He listened dully to his father's voice.

'Hello there . . . No, don't worry . . . Yes, there is a meeting tomorrow . . . I'll soon sort him out for you, you can be sure of that . . . That's right, nobody stands in my way. I thought everyone knew that by now . . . I'll rattle his cage as soon as the meeting begins . . . Tomorrow then, breakfast at seven, I'll tell you then how we can get rid of him.'

'Hi, son.' John's father invaded the dim orderly half light of John's room, a big smile creasing his face as he approached John. He demolished half of John's protective nest and the two stuffed dogs fell silently on to the thick carpet as he sat on John's bed. John looked at him with a tense and worried expression. His father swept some toy soldiers to the floor as he spoke. 'School OK? Any tests today?' He did not wait for an answer. 'Come out top?' John's father saw life as a simple matter

41

of winning and losing, profit or loss. John took in a sharp breath. He had a stock of ready-made answers designed to get rid of his father.

'No tests. But I scored a goal in football.' This was a lie but John knew it was his duty to report a minor triumph. Such a lie could not be checked out and his father would leave the room contented for the time being.

'That's the way. Now get some sleep, son. Don't forget it's tomorrow they check you out and see if you're ready for your next belt. I'll be there to give you a cheer. Goodnight. God bless, son.' Then he was gone, leaving the air fragrant and disturbed. Expensive cologne was one of Mr Snow's tactics for being thought about when he had left the room.

Sleep abandoned John. Downstairs he heard the chink of glasses and the loud talk of his parents. This case won, that contract won, that opposing solicitor made to look a fool, that rival told to clear his desk and get lost, that client told exactly what to do, the Board told precisely what they should do next . . . John sighed as he heard the fragments of it all drift up to his room.

Eventually he got out of his ruined nest and padded softly into his bathroom which was en suite with his bedroom. He was hot, he needed some fresh air. He put the lid of the lavatory down, kneeled on it, and began to undo the catches and burglar locks on the window. The hardwood window protested a little as it opened. Mrs Snow feared burglaries and monitored window opening in the house.

John felt the rush of cold clean night air on his face. He leaned out eagerly. It was dark but there was still the ghost of the sunset and a thin moon, as finely lined as if it had been done with a sharp gold pencil. The moon almost sat on the horizon and there was a sprinkling of stars. John gulped at the sweet air and stared at the trees where the moon sat. That was where he would take Sam Wilkinson.

John became calmer and dreamier as the air softly blew about him. His mind relaxed and he retrieved a favourite memory which he often did on the few times he was happy. One night, in Spain, his parents had had a party and drunk too much. John had escaped from the large white villa and had begun to climb the hill behind the house with its walled garden and fountains. Higher and higher John had climbed, in a wild race with the sun that was trying to set far across the blue sea. He had raced the sunset to the top of the hill where he found a large flat space. There had been a crowd of Spanish boys playing football under the dark warm blue sky. John had joined in, not caring, for the first time in his life, whether he lost or won. He had played till the first stars came out, not wanting to walk through the wrought-iron gate of the villa ever again.

Since that day he had promised himself he would escape again. One day he would have freedom. He leaned out further into the welcoming night, night that seemed to encourage his plans for escape and for Sam.

John's house was near the crest of a hill. Below John's house and two other big houses, smaller houses stretched in mazes of streets and roads, trees and parks, down to the distant town in the river valley. On the flat top of the hill had once stood a large Victorian house, Topwood Grange, surrounded by its own parkland. The old crumbling mansion had been bought by the local council in 1960 and demolished. In its place they had built a block of council flats four storeys high. For various reasons the flats were unpopular. There was no proper bus service, they looked out to rather bleak empty hill country, winter snowfall was heavy, and the school was a mile away. Now the flats were boarded up and soon to be demolished.

John was aware that his father hated the flats. For a time the council had placed 'problem' families in them. This had infuriated John's parents who did not want 'drop-outs', 'drug addicts', or 'misfits' anywhere near them. They had arranged endless meetings and petitions, had become friendly with an MP, and finally the council closed the flats. Once again John's parents celebrated a victory, a battle won. John knew his father wanted the old parkland to build 'executive' six bedroomed houses and extend their own garden to take in the view. He knew he would buy it and get it. John smiled to the night. The old flats were part of his fantasy.

During the campaign to evict the 'problems', John's father had mysteriously obtained two keys to two flats that had been seriously vandalized. Pictures appeared in the local and national papers. HALF A MILLION WASTED ON LAYABOUTS, shouted one paper. At the peak of the campaign John had taken one of the keys. It was not even missed in the excitement. One day, he had thought, he would escape, live in a flat, independent, like the men in the videos, in charge of everything and everybody.

Already he had secretly taken food, a little at a time so his mother would suspect nothing. He had a bag packed full of old clothes. In the flats he would be in charge of his own life and in control of others. John knew the teenage gang used the flats for smoking and drinking and messing about in, but they would be no problem. They seemed friendly whenever he saw them. He had plenty of money to buy them what they wanted.

They would not say he was hiding there or care what he was doing with others.

By now the moon had quietly slipped behind the thick trees of the Grange's parkland. John shut the window and the whispered rustling of the trees and the sweet cold air were shut out. John felt he could sleep now. He climbed back into bed and rearranged the toy nest. He dimmed the light to its lowest setting—he hated absolute darkness. In one bag he had hidden for his escape were several torches and packets of the fine wax candles his mother used for her dinner parties. John sighed and leaned back, still staring in the direction of Sam's and smiling a little.

SIX

It was one of the mysteries of the universe, thought Sam, how things went wrong together. Horrible things never spaced themselves out neatly, like the planets round the sun. If you could be bullied for a day, have a rest from it for a day, then lose your best friend, have a good day, then lose your pocket money then have another good day, it might be bearable. But life was not like that. Today had shown that clearly. John had threatened him, Adam had ignored him, the phone call had scared him to death, and now the family were picking on him.

'You're very quiet, Sam,' said his father. His father was edgy himself and so was quick to spot it in others. He had been told today that there was a strong chance he would be redundant by the end of the week. 'I said, "You're very quiet, Sam".' He was irritably eager for a reply.

'He should be quiet,' said his mother. She still felt tired and bothered by the £5.98 she had been short in her till. Fatigue made her nag. 'He's worrying over that jacket we bought from Marks & Sparks. He won't wear it. Came home soaked to the skin.'

'It's a pity he's nothing else to worry him,' said his father bleakly, talking as though Sam was not in the room. Worry made him sound harsh although in reality he was a kind and gentle man. He took a gulp of tea. 'He should be worrying over something that matters like cleaning the rabbits out.'

Sam's middle brother Richard was quick to sense the

dice were loaded against Sam. He spoke in a superior way to his mother.

'I cleaned them out last week and the Thursday before that. It's definitely his turn.'

Sam stared at them all. He hated it when they talked as if he wasn't there. And he felt the day slipping into even worse disasters.

'And heaven alone knows what you were doing in that shower,' continued his mother. She passed her hand over her forehead. 'When I went in there was enough water to float Noah and his Ark on. You must have stood in the shower with the curtain out thinking about that jacket—'

Sam got to his feet. 'I'm going to clean out the rabbits and I hope it makes everyone very happy,' he shouted. He slammed the door as he left the room and headed down the garden. The dragon of discontent filled his mind with the thought that everything had always gone wrong for him—ever since the day he was left like a cuckoo's egg on the steps. It was very unusual for the dragon to breathe misery twice in one day but today had been especially bad.

It continued. Nero, the black rabbit, escaped. Being unhappy made Sam careless. Nero made for the only hole in the garden fence that attracted him as surely as a magnet pulls at a pin. Sam watched dejectedly as Nero vanished neatly into Mrs Stevens's garden. She was waiting for him when he had gone all the way round to her house. Nero had done his worst and Mrs Stevens said it did not matter but Sam sensed it mattered a very great deal.

'You'll have to tell Mummy there'll be no fresh sprouts for your Christmas dinner, Sammy. Bunny's just eaten the lot. And they were doing so well. He's taken the tops off the lot. Well, that's life, I suppose. At least it's not an earthquake or a bomb.'

She held up a beheaded sprout plant and regarded it sadly through her bifocals, her head tilted back a little to focus on the misery. She gave a dry mirthless chuckle and Sam knew that sprouts were as important as bombs and earthquakes.

Sam did not inform his mother about the coming problems concerning Christmas dinner. Instead he whistled for Spot, his dog. He was fed up with the day and wanted to get to bed. Usually he left taking Spot out as late as he could get away with. He liked to walk in the dark with Spot and scan the skies for UFOs and meteors. But he was unhappy tonight. And at the back of his mind was the thought that John might creep from his bed, escape the house, and get him. He tried telling himself that this was unlikely for John was kept very busy and Sam knew Mr and Mrs Snow rarely let John out even on to the road.

Sam carefully avoided going near John's house. He was taking no risks. But this was a nuisance. The darkest part of the sky was over the countryside behind John's house. Before tonight Sam had been happy to go beyond John's house and into the overgrown grounds of the flats. He was not supposed to go there in the dark but he liked the darkness and Spot liked the smells from the rabbits and foxes that lived in the dense bushes and thickets.

Tonight, Sam kept away and walked the lighted streets. He wondered if John had his den somewhere in the grounds. Sam then hurried an astonished Spot homewards. The dog was bemused. He was used to long explorations of burrows and tunnels under the vegetation, while his master stared up to the sky.

Sam sighed with relief when he reached his room. Surely, he thought, he was safe at last. The first thing he did, as he relaxed a little, was to set up his telescope. This was a long white tube that he focused on the night sky and scanned it for stars and any other wonders. It always pleased Sam that his room faced away from the city and towards John's house and darkness. Light pollution from the town made the southern sky impossible to view. But over the northern and western hills and John's house, darkness reigned supreme.

Sam felt the tension drain from him as he unscrewed the lens cap of this, his most prized possession. Although the telescope showed everything upside down, it was powerful and showed Saturn's rings and the shadows on the moon, made by its jagged crater edges. At first the cheap telescope, showing moon and planets upside down, had troubled Sam. Then he realized there was no upside down in space and the universe. It was an Earthling's idea. He put an eye to the lens.

It was a clear night and he focused on the tip of the crescent moon. John was forgotten. His space books and the telescope always worked this special brand of magic. He stared for a long time at the sunlit craters on the moon where dawn was just breaking, the sun rising over those endless craters. One hundred miles along the moon's surface it was still in night, lit by earthlight, a greenish glow that always thrilled Sam. He suddenly left the telescope and found the map of the night sky for September that came free with a magazine he bought every month. Yes! It would be worth searching for Mercury tonight. He had never found this most elusive of planets. The map said the planet was visible for one hour after sunset in the constellation of Virgo. Sam adjusted the telescope.

It made up for the worst day of his life so far—except the day he was laid on the hospital steps. He spotted Mercury, smaller than Venus, a tiny tiny half moon like a fragment of scintillating mirror, reflecting the harsh light of the nearby sun. Sam sucked in his mouth and stared and stared. The planet was sinking fast down towards a distant wood on the far hills. Sam sighed with pleasure. He had seen all the planets now except Pluto. He watched the planet plunge into the tangle of the wood, wink and glitter, and then vanish from his gaze.

But still he kept his eye to the telescope and looked at the stars in Virgo. Somewhere he had read that in this group of stars was a vast greedy cannibal star, a giant black hole, eight hundred light years across, a cannibal that had sucked in billions of stars to their death. But what if it kept on growing and swallowed up more and more stars and finally the whole universe itself? For some reason this made him think of John and he nudged the telescope.

He continued to look and wished he hadn't. There, in the circle of focus was John, propped up in a nest of pillows, very faint and dim, but certainly John. John, looking like someone's mad fantasy of the Man in the Moon. Or like the god of some distant cold planet, a parasitic god, that covered the entirety of the planet's surface. Sam licked his lips which suddenly felt very dry and flaked with salt. But he had to keep staring. Then he was reminded of a reference book that he had looked at that very afternoon, a book that showed an illustration of an unhatched cuckoo still imprisoned in its egg. John looked, viewed in the circle of the telescope, like some space monster that might at any moment break out and hatch into something that would do nothing but harm to Sam.

Sam's dad came into the room. He had been cleaning the car and the fresh air and routine task had calmed him down. He had seen Sam's light and had come up to see him. He was shocked at what he saw.

'You look white, Sam. You OK?'

'Yes . . . yes, thanks. Yes, I'm all right.' He swallowed, for his throat had gone dry. 'I've just discovered Mercury and now . . . it's gone.'

His father gave him a quick hug. Ever since he and his wife had adopted Sam, he had always felt that Sam needed special watching over. He lacked the resilience of Richard and James, his own natural sons. He squeezed Sam's shoulder. 'Well, get into bed now. You look as if you could use a good night's sleep. I'll bring you up a drink of hot chocolate.'

He found Sam still sitting on the edge of the bed when he returned ten minutes later with a beaker full of hot steaming chocolate.

'Come on then, Sam, into bed now.'

Fifteen minutes later, Sam was still to be seen sitting on the edge of his bed, deep in thought. But he wasn't thinking of the tiny planet dazzled with the sun, or of the mysteries of the stars. He was thinking of John. That dim image on the telescope, like some evil force from beyond, was invading his being, sucking all the will out of him, paralysing him with a cold fear until he was as cold as the beaker of chocolate left on his bedside table.

SEVEN

John's mother seated herself at the head of the massive kitchen table next morning and watched John eat his breakfast. Her arms rested lightly on the wooden surface and she looked not unlike a critical judge in chambers. John was eating his low-fat breakfast cereal and sorting through a pile of letters. His mother watched as keenly as a trial judge watches a prisoner. Each letter was a square parchment envelope with the name of a boy printed on it with the immaculate precision of the law firm's best printer. Inside the envelope was a sheet of A4 legal vellum, the very best the office had, inviting every boy in the class to John's forthcoming birthday party. An invitation to every boy—except Sam.

'Are you quite sure there are fourteen boys in your class excluding yourself?'

'Yes.'

'Are you sure? I seem to remember Mrs Firth telling me last July, when I was introduced to her, that there would be sixteen boys in the class. Not counting you, my chicken, that makes fifteen. Are you sure you have invited every boy in the class?'

'Yes.' John was as short and snappish as he dared be. His mother had her nose into everything.

'Let me check my school governor's disk.' She made as if to move to a computer terminal built into one of the kitchen surfaces. 'My Kitchen Site', she called it.

'A boy left, Mum.'

'Why?'

Mrs Snow liked to know every detail of the school

52

she governed. And firing questions in court had become a habit out of court. She prided herself on her excellence as an interrogator.

'His dad got another job in another town.' John was becoming pink with the exertion of lying.

'Who did? What were they called?'

'Thomas Whittaker . . . his dad . . . Thomas'sss . . . Tom.' John stammered and spluttered. Thomas had left at Spring Bank Holiday because of John's secret and merciless bullying. 'Mrs Firth probably had an old class list that wasn't altered.' He needed to lie to get fourteen letters. John was now an unlovely shade of boiled ham pink.

'Of course.' A hand sparkling with rings waved assent and agreement. 'His father was a client of mine and suddenly he would have no more to do with me because I was a governor of the school. He refused to tell me why he left the district and school. But I shall find out. I always do.'

John fled to punish the bacteria in his mouth. He cleaned his teeth upstairs with savage fury. He returned downstairs zipping up his anorak and swinging his expensive sports bag. His mother still looked thoughtful much to John's alarm. He dug in his pocket and found a school letter to give to her that he had forgotten to give her earlier. Letters from school always diverted her away from dangerous topics.

'Here, Mum. Forgot to give you this.' She took a letter from him on bright yellow paper and frowned. John's colour returned to off-white and he visibly relaxed. He vaguely wondered if he ought to keep a store of such letters for difficult moments.

'Thank you, chick. What a tatty letter. I really must have a word with Nancy Highfield about the quality of

53

letters she sends to parents. The school needs a new photocopier. I must talk to your father. Perhaps his office will be throwing one out soon that the school could have.'

She made her way to the back door leaving an intense vapour trail of Chanel perfume. John followed her, as silently and obediently as her own sharp shadow did down the garden path to the garages. He stood passively by as she reached in her bag for the tiny keyboard. He watched her key in a number and point the keyboard to the back door that locked itself promptly. She opened the garage with the same sure movements.

Every morning John's mother took him to school in her newest car. This was highly convenient for her as the senior partners in her firm did not arrive until ten. Going early to work enabled her to do some case work, have coffee with the partners, see clients, lunch with the partners, then return home to John. Other well-oiled arrangements were made for when she was in court. He was taken to the gym with his father, or to martial arts. Mrs Snow smiled a smile of sheer self confidence as she drove along the streets to school.

'Out you get, my chicken.'

John got out. She watched him with the eye of a mother hawk, fierce and protective and intensely caring, as John walked to the school gates with his bundle of letters. As she watched a small sigh breathed from her carefully lipsticked lips and her expression softened. John, judges, drunken drivers, child abusers, thieves, who were all terrified of her in the courtroom, would all have been amazed at the look on her face. She genuinely loved John with a ferocity that filled her whole being. She planned that John should have nothing but the very best in life. Everything she did for John was truly done for what she believed was his best interests. Parties, expensive gymnasiums, low fat cereals, diet sausages were all aimed at John as a result of her motherly love. It was the one thing that kept her going, gave her the boundless energy that so astonished the other barristers she knew. Very few people guessed that she loved John so much. John himself would not have understood it if he had known. He just considered his mother as the biggest nuisance in his life. What she thought was care, he considered as pestering.

Nothing had ever stood in the way of her maternal love for John. Nothing—not even his natural father. Soon after John had been born she had decided that life with her first husband, John's natural father, simply was not good enough for Baby John. She knew that he would never be able to provide for her and the baby the very best things in life. Charming, handsome, scatterbrained, a spendthrift, she knew he was a poor provider of the good things in life. So she had left him, taking Baby John of course.

John's happy-go-lucky natural father had known better than to challenge her in the courts for his baby son. Then she had married the very rich man whom John now called father. He had been a client of hers and he was all the things she wanted in a father for John.

The new rich husband had adopted John. The new Mrs Snow was highly satisfied with the new nest she had chosen for her chick.

Mrs Snow's dreamy thoughts were shattered by a Year Six girl whizzing by the gleaming car on a skateboard. The girl had missed the car's polished lustre by millimetres. The girl—Mrs Snow's face hardened into judgemental criticism—was blowing a swaying bubble of chemical pink bubble gum. The bubble shattered as the girl shot through the school gate with incredible speed. Mrs Snow matched the action by whipping out her electronic notebook, keying in SC/G. She rattled the keys fiercely as she keyed a quick memo for Mrs Highfield. Her secretary would fax her discontent later. (The school fax machine was a redundant model from her own office.) Mrs Snow slid the electronic notebook back in her case, switched on the engine, and glided away from the school. The splendid car was almost noiseless. There was just a soft sigh of air as though large wings had just departed.

John lurked in the entrance till the bell rang then he made his way to the cloakroom. He had a smile on his face remarkably like his mother's. He made his way to the classroom with the bundle of letters, walking a little faster than he normally did. When he reached the classroom door Mrs Firth bustled out, speaking loudly. 'Reading books out and *quickly* please. I must just fly to the photocopier. There's been a queue since eight o'clock. Settle down. I'll be back in a tick.' John watched her thunder down the corridor and his mouth stretched into an unlovely grin.

John pushed his way to the trays and handed out the envelopes to the boys in the class. They were impressed by the sight of their names and addresses printed on the dazzling large envelopes. They were even more impressed by the letter, inviting them by name, to attend John's birthday party at a well known and expensive restaurant, followed by a visit to a leisure centre. This promised ten-pin bowling and simulated games with lasers and other electronic wonders. Every boy felt the crisp paper in his hand, every boy felt a thrill of pleasure and expectation. Only Sam was unable to enjoy Mrs Snow's bounty.

The noise round the trays in the classroom became uproar. The boys became wild with excitement and began pushing. John was smiling in the centre of this whirling excitement. Caroline, struggling to get her tray out from between two boys, yanked crossly and the whole tray shot out and spilled her books on to the floor. Her pencil case landed at John's feet and he promptly put a heavy foot on it, cracking several pens inside it.

'Sorry, Caroline,' said John very loudly as Mrs Firth rushed back holding copies still hot from the copier. She gave John an encouraging smile thinking he was still doing his best to socialize.

'Come along now. Sit down quickly and quietly. That means you, Nathan. Why you are jumping up and down with an envelope between your teeth escapes me. It's a what? An invite to a booze up? Don't be *so silly, Nathan.*' Her voice became cutting and the children fell and flopped into their chairs. 'I want you all reading as quietly and sensibly as Sam is doing at his table.'

Silence developed. She sat at her desk and put on her glasses and made a note for herself to put on John's record how well he was mixing with the class, and how immature Nathan was. She watched John over the top of her glasses. John was even smiling as he leaned over Sam Wilkinson to get a book from the poetry display she had set up before school had begun. How nice it was to see John smiling and saying something friendly to Sam Wilkinson. Sam did not share her enthusiasm, as John spoke unpleasantly into his ear.

'I've forgotten to invite you to my party. But I've not forgotten yesterday. I've got my plans made for you. So maybe you'll not be needing an invite anyway. Maybe you'll be some place else.' John had slipped back to mid-Atlantic video speak. He walked back to his place with a swagger not unlike his father when he first got out of a new car he had bought.

Mrs Firth liked the class to read while she did the register and ensured she had everything she needed for her carefully planned day. Most mornings she was busy with planning notes, children's progress profiles, and various notebooks of her own. She called this twenty minutes 'free reading'. Busy with a dozen different things she did not notice John's strange reading habits. John was not what she would have called a 'good' reader. In fact he found reading painfully and annoyingly hard. He would not admit this and to hide the fact from himself he read the same books every morning. These books were the ones he knew by heart. Surrounded by such books he did not have to face up to the fact that he could not read easily.

Every morning he read his old friend *The Owl Who Was Afraid of the Dark*. After a chapter of Plop's adventures he turned to Jan Pieńkowski's *Easter Story*. It managed to blow John's mind every morning as he looked at Jesus nailed to a cross of wood. It was beyond John's understanding to see why Jesus, with all the power of God behind him, had allowed such a thing to happen. Then he would look at *Willy the Champ* by Anthony Brown. He liked the way Willy made himself a champion by body building. John could understand why he did that.

During maths, while Mrs Firth was busy with a group who were further on than he was, John pretended to fetch a calculator. He had a perfectly good one in his pencil case but he felt the need to torment Sam again. Passing Sam's table he snatched at the giant plastic novelty paper clip that Sam used to clip together his maths project. It was bright pink plastic and also a ball point pen. John straightened it out so it was a metre in length and waved it in the air like a wobbly wand. Adam and Mark laughed loudly and encouragingly.

'Don't be so silly over there,' said Mrs Firth, not looking up from a problem about a pyramid. It was very important that her top maths group did well so that the school average could be kept high. But Sam was so angry he called out.

'Mrs Firth, Mrs Firth, John's messing with my paper clip.'

John reacted with amazing and remarkable speed and bent the clip back to its original shape.

'I was only looking,' said John with an injured tone. He nodded encouragingly to Mrs Firth in the way his father did to his workmen. Mrs Firth stood up and looked crossly towards them. But her mind was full of obtuse angles and she saw the paper clip once again on Sam's table.

'Concentrate on your work, John, not plastic paper clips.' She subsided again, frowning as she tore off the angles of a pyramid's base to prove they added up to the three hundred and sixty of a circle. 'Close your mouth, Jack, and watch me,' she said crossly. Her group seemed far more interested in John than pyramidal angles.

Sam felt isolated and alone, the feeling of abandonment smoking into his brain. All the vitality drained from him, just like the spring had vanished from the paper clip. The paper clip looked normal enough but it now held the papers slackly. Since John had touched it, it was not the same. Sam was like his paper clip. Some hidden part of him was destroyed.

Slowly the day became worse. At dinnertime the other boys crowded round John and talked excitedly about the coming party. Sam was abandoned and isolated. To pass the time he wandered off into the boys' toilets, planning to make his visit last as long as he could. He leant against a wall and was found there by Mrs Bright, a dinner lady.

'Come out of there at once. I expect you're one of those silly boys who unravels toilet rolls for the fun of it.'

Sam left her to her mutterings and strolled slowly over to the nature area where you were supposed to sit still and quietly. He stared into the distance towards the dustbins. He wondered if he should hide in one of them. He would be better off in one, he thought. Thomas had hidden from John in there to escape John's long silent stares. John had never actually touched or said anything to Thomas. He had watched him, stared at him, swaggered past him, wildly jealous of Thomas's ability in football.

In the afternoon Mrs Firth decided to give the class what she described as a treat in the games lesson. 'For two weeks we have been working very hard with our throwing and catching skills. I'd like to organize a class rounders game. Adam and Caroline get your heads together and make a team. Jane and John you do the same. Equal numbers of boys and girls in each, please.'

The chosen captains began calling out names. Sam was well known for excellent fielding and fast running and expected to be chosen by Adam and Caroline. But after much whispering, cross looks from Caroline and Jane, warning glowerings from John, Sam was not chosen. He was left unselected and Mrs Firth told Sam sharply to go into Adam's team 'to make even numbers'. She spoke irritably as though Sam was to blame for the delay.

Competitive team games put an unbearable strain on John. He could not cope with losing. Moreover he was not good at planning where his team should stand and field. His team scored a pitiful two rounders and it became obvious they were the losing side. John began to turn an unpleasant shade of shellfish pink. The pink flushed to a dangerous red when Adam and Caroline scored a rounder each and Sam took the bat. Sam swiped the ball into the nettle and bramble patch of the nature area.

'Well played, Sam,' called Mrs Firth. 'But we can't get the ball out of there. You'll have to take your turn again with a new ball.'

She threw a ball to Jane the bowler. John began to swell with venom and hatred like a rattlesnake before a bite. Sam whacked the new ball and John's hopelessly organized field scampered in all directions to chase it. Sam raced round the posts twice and gave Adam and Caroline a clear lead. John, unable to look defeat in the face, erupted and spluttered.

'That's not fair,' he yelled. 'That was with the new ball. It's a better ball than the one we had. The fact that Sam Wilkinson, of all people, could score a double shows it's a better ball.'

'That's quite enough!' shouted Mrs Firth. 'Carry on the game. All the team must have a go.'

John clearly saw that he would be, as his father would say, 'thrashed'. He was clearly going to lose by a large margin. He took disruptive action at once.

'That's not fair. You've given the other team an advantage. It's—'

Mrs Firth reacted exactly as he had hoped. John had had many years of turning teachers' rages to his advantage. She put her whistle to her lips and blew till her face was as red as the plums in a neighbouring garden. The quivering of the gold ponies registered her anger.

'The whole class will go inside now. I will not be told what is fair and unfair by children in my own class. Who do they think they are? How dare they!'

John smirked. He had dared. And the game was now neither won nor lost by his reckoning. The class were hustled inside and given a sharp lecture on fair play and how to lose and never mind what they saw on television or on football fields. Did they hear? Mrs Firth's plum-red rage raged till hometime. She expected John to begin a roll-around under the tables as she aimed most of her lecture in his direction. But John did not want to be sent home. That was not in his plans for Sam Wilkinson. Instead he remained on his chair, with a half smile on his face that Mrs Firth could not decide was either polite or repentant. It was neither.

Mrs Firth hammered home the importance and advantages of fair play and being able to lose. 'And now nobody has won because nobody would lose. What a wasted afternoon.' John's grin widened with pleasure. He had won. He had stopped Sam winning. If he himself could not win, then, to use his father's words used so often in John's house, he would 'make damn sure nobody else takes the goodies'.

'I hope I shall not have to say this again,' concluded Mrs Firth, still glowing with fury. 'If people won't lose nobody will play again. I shall see to that.'

'Suits me,' said John under his breath but loud enough for Adam and his admirers to hear. Adam gave him a smile acknowledging John's daring cheek. Mrs Firth thought it wise to pretend not to hear. She had just had what she considered her first battle with John and she thought she had done rather well. After all, he was still upright. Other teachers had warned her he would be chewing the carpet if she told him off for too long. Her face lightened to a delicate raspberry.

'Put your things away and stand quietly by your tables until the bell.'

'And as for you, Wilkinson, you're dead meat,' said John to Sam in the bustle of putting away books. 'I'm having all my friends round tomorrow night to my place. They're my gang now. I'm going to share a few secret plans with them. You might as well cease to exist now.'

Sam asked Mrs Firth, now a relaxed rose pink, if he could go to the toilets. He made a wild dash out of school and ran all the way home as he had never run before.

EIGHT

The birthday party was a huge success. John thought it was and so did his mother. She had invited all the parents of the boys that had been invited. She liked to be part of the community, she told her friends. The grown-ups sat at a long table with Mr Snow buying beer at one end and Mrs Snow pouring wine at the other. John and his friends sat a little distance away. Everyone seemed to be having a wonderful time.

John, just out of earshot of his parents, just out of sight behind a pillar entwined with plants, seized the opportunity to do things his mother stopped him from doing. He ordered two helpings of fries and organized a competition to see how much could be stuffed into the mouth at once. The sight of John with bulging cheeks and popping eyes like a Disney chick, caused much laughter. He swallowed a glass of non-diet Coke and then belched softly and continually for twenty seconds like the deep rumbling note of a church organ.

Discovering these forbidden activities caused wide-spread and admiring laughter, John advanced to spitting out things he did not like. Lettuce fragments and cucumber hit the polished table with a defiant and triumphant splat. Adam choked with laughter and John became the mirror image of his father, clapping Adam on his back just as his father was clapping Adam's father on the back after telling a very rude joke.

John had never been so much the centre of attention and laughter—even if some of the boys' laughter had been a little nervous. As the meal progressed John seemed to grow larger, like a worm-stuffed baby bird in its nest. He flapped his arms around and his voice became strident and coarse and eventually reached the ears of his mother. She walked over with smiling nonchalance that fooled everyone except John. The boys thought she had just walked over to see if they were enjoying themselves.

'Don't excite yourself too much, darling. We don't want tears before bedtime to spoil your special day, do we?'

For a time these precise, carefully chosen words sobered John. He knew when he changed from a chick to a darling trouble threatened. 'Tears before bedtime' meant exactly what it said—there would be tears if he did not behave. Yet, when the heels of his mother had tapped their precise journey back to the other parents, John saw the admiring looks of the other boys upon him. He became filled with a curious surge of power as if electricity had been switched on inside a powerful machine. John felt in charge. He felt a sense of power. He felt that anything was possible and that all his plans for escape and for Wilkinson would come true. He felt he could tackle anything and anybody. Perhaps this very night was the time for the plan, he thought, repeating the mouth-stuffing trick to make the others laugh. Adam laughed until his ribs ached and he got a painful stitch. Tonight's the night, thought John, performing another amazing organ rumble of a belch, more felt than heard by the others. It was a wonderful party. They all said so.

'And as for you, Sam Wilkinson, you're dead meat. I'm having everyone round to my house tomorrow night. They're my gang now. You're as good as dead when I get you.'

Sam had raced home with the words that John had been using the last days shouting in his brain. They kept on repeating themselves, loudly, like someone shouting on a mountainside and causing an avalanche. Sam could feel the whole of his world slipping away from underneath him. Each minute that passed made the voice of John seem louder and gave the impression his life was on the move downwards to some capture and disaster. The feelings in Sam were so strong that when he finally made it home he was sick on the back door step.

His father was seriously alarmed. His worst fears had been realized and he had been told there was no more work for him. He had been in the kitchen preparing the meal and worrying over how money would be found for all the bills. But the sight of Sam being ill lifted him clear of his anxieties. Sam had, as he explained to his wife later, 'looked like death'. Sam was made to go straight to bed. Sam did as he was told and in bed wondered if this was what old people felt like when they said they wanted to die.

The woman he called 'Gran', the mother of his adoptive mother, had had cancer and been in great pain. She had loved Sam and Sam had loved her and he had insisted on going to see her in the hospital. He had heard her say 'There's no point to living like this'. And now for the first time in his life Sam understood why some people no longer wish to keep on living. There was no point to living when you had no friends, nobody to laugh with, play a game with, go home with, phone up or swap things with—or even laugh at teachers with.

Like his Gran's illness, John's threats felt like a vast sickening pain. He felt he was utterly out of control and could feel his life sliding away at a dizzy speed. To be awake was a nightmare. Sleep did not help. John and his shouting voice leapt at him as soon as he awoke.

Sam was ordered to stay in bed the next day. Both his mum and dad were worried over the white face of Sam as he lay in his bed. Sam's face had a lifeless look that scared his mother. She thought of calling the doctor but she was not sure what to say to her. She would wait a day or two. But she was very worried. And Sam found for the very first time in his life nothing in his room comforted him or cheered him. John's threats had invaded Sam's brain with the efficiency of warlike aliens in a computer game. All life and hope had been savagely eclipsed.

At teatime, after he had spent a full day in bed, his father shouted him downstairs. If Sam could not make it he was going to ring the doctor and say it was an emergency. Sam did make it but flopped sadly in front of the television. His father made a huge effort to be cheerful and try to rouse Sam.

'I've just been talking to Adam's dad when I went down to the post office. He told me all the boys are going with the Snows to this posh restaurant that has just opened. John's birthday or something.' He looked at Sam enquiringly. Sam stared at the television without seeing it. John's presence in his brain was like a black hole, sucking everything into nothingness. 'Adam's dad asked if I was going because the Snows had invited all the mums and dads too. I told him you were ill and I knew nothing about it and you must have forgotten to give me the invitation.' He turned away and lit the oven. 'He said he was sure we could go without you. But of course I'm not going if you're not. Then they're going to the leisure centre at Bunjy's. A shame to have missed that though. They've got just about everything there.' He concentrated on taking the wrapping off something and preparing it for the oven.

It seemed to Sam that a ray of warm sunshine shone into the cold darkness of his brain. Bunjy's with its bowling alleys and laser games and swimming pools was miles and miles away across the town. It would be very late when John returned home. It would be perfectly safe to go out with Spot on his usual walk. Sam visibly brightened as he wondered if John's latest threats were simply John shooting his big mouth off yet again. He looked away from the small screen of the portable television to see his father watching him intently.

'You've got a bit of colour back in your cheeks, Sam. Tea won't be long. A shame to miss a free visit to Bunjy's. I could leave this lot in the oven for the others. Shall I phone the Snows?'

'I'm not bothered,' said Sam in a small voice, the beam of sunlight in his mind dying and plunging everything back to gloom. 'No. I'll not go.'

'I didn't know we were supposed to be going until I saw Adam's dad,' said his father, this time with a hint of accusation in his tone.

Sam was saved by the bleeping of the timer. He got up and walked to the window. The sky was clearing, clouds were blowing away on a cheerful mischievous wind that ruffled puddles of sky reflected blue. Sam laughed as the wind lifted a carrier bag and made a cat run across the road. For the first time in twenty-four hours his mind cleared itself of threats and imprisonment. John was out of the way for the night. He could stargaze when it was dark.

'Is it ready yet?' he suddenly asked his dad. 'I'm hungry. I've not eaten properly since breakfast yesterday.'

It was dark when a procession of cars arrived at the Snow's big house. The proceedings had gone as Mrs Snow had planned. The four hours from four until eight that she had planned to focus on John with quality time were over. She had some court notes to read over but she allowed another hour to socialize with John's friends' parents. She felt an hour with her neighbours would be very profitable. There were several things she wanted to organize at school and to make sure she got her own way in meetings, coffee with the parents would be marvellous preparation.

She rapidly keyed in the code of the door opening and burglar alarm then flew round the house switching on lamps, lighting fires, and turning on soft happy music. She ground some coffee beans so that when her husband and the other parents made a slower entry they would be welcomed by the smell of fresh coffee. They would then be unable to resist the invitation to stay for a coffee and a chat. Just an hour, she thought, as she smilingly told everyone that coffee was almost ready. She issued a charming smile as the soft leather furniture and feather cushions of the lounge gently captured the parents.

'Mum, can we go out for a run round and fun?' John stood before his mother like a supplicant in court. She studied him thoughtfully. He's suddenly different, she thought. His usual pale face was flushed with a good colour. His eyes were bright and alert and sparkling. He looked intelligent. His hair was properly brushed and styled. He looked alive and vital, the sort of son she wanted, a go-getter, out to take what the world could give. A wave of love rocked her organized mind.

Normally she would never have let him out when it was dark. She had seen and heard in court the fearful things that happened to children who were allowed to wander about as they chose. She was convinced the streets and countryside were no longer safe for children. But surely, she thought, looking at John's eager face, there would be no harm with fourteen other boys. And it would mean space and quiet for coffee and persuasion. It would enable her to bring up the topic of that dreadful male teacher who had thrown John out of the school team. She wanted him to be the teacher to go when necessary cuts were made in the next budget. She gave John and the boys a warm smile.

'Of course, my chick. But for no longer than one hour. And you must all stay together.'

The other boys who had crowded into the large kitchen smiled innocently at Mrs Snow. Like her son she looked like someone who had the power.

'Wait a mo,' said John breathlessly. 'I'll get a torch and the—some things . . .' He'd nearly given himself away.

There was the sound of muffled thunder as he pounded up the thick carpet of the stairs. Then Mrs Snow watched them all vanish into the twilight garden and she smiled indulgently as she carried her Crown Derby coffee pots into the lounge to impress the parents.

In the garden John crowed loudly like an escaped cock chicken. It was a call of sheer pleasure, power, and joy. A fresh night wind rustled the topmost leaves of the trees and a few fluttered down in the growing darkness. A plump crescent moon shone brightly in the remains of an autumn sunset. John whooped loudly and checked he had the key to the flats in his pocket. This was life! This was freedom! This was like living in a video.

He led the boys to the top of the garden where a deep shrubbery of trees and a thick hedge had been planted by Mrs Snow. This barrier of dense jungle had been planted to stop 'them' from getting in the garden or looking in. To emphasize the fact there was a perimeter fence of concrete posts and barbed wire beyond the hedge. The flats had been an alien state to Mrs Snow. This was her Berlin Wall.

'Come on. Follow me.' John crawled on hands and knees on the bone dry earth under the conifers, fragrant with the smell of soil and evergreens. The earthy smell made him wilder still. The distant security lights filtered through and made the boys look like hunting tigers as they poured through the narrow tunnel. They, too, shared John's rising excitement, for like John most were not allowed out after nightfall. They all crawled through a hole in the fence that John had carefully concealed from his mother with a tangle of ivy and branches. Then the ordered density of the Snow's garden was left behind and they were in the tangled chaos of the grounds belonging to the flats. Reaching a clearing John stood in the thin blue moonlight breathing heavily. He was as intoxicated with freedom as he had been that night in Spain when he had escaped.

'My den's in there. I'll show you. Only my best friends know and they're older than you lot.' He thought of the teenage boys who had delivered the papers. They had become his friends in his mind. He said no more but led the way towards the flats, pushing through overgrown trees and brambles.

The other boys became silent. So, it was true then. He did have a den here. And he must have older friends from outside school. They knew nobody had ever been his special friend in school. They were unaware of John's fantasy world. They followed him not saying a word.

They all kept together, the boys following John obediently. It was a dream come true for him. John moved forward in the pale, thin, cold moonlight and he left footsteps in the faint white dew that was falling. The scene was like that of an exciting film. They could hear John's heavy breathing. An owl hooted somewhere in the trees and a dog barked in reply and several of them jumped at the sound. High in the royal blue of the sky they could see a moving star, perhaps an aeroplane, a satellite or perhaps not . . . mystery and a sense of expectation shivered in the air in company with the frosty moon.

The flats crouched ahead, derelict, silent and almost impossible to distinguish against the dark blue sky. They heard the confident click of John's torch and saw the powerful beam of white light feel its way over the cracking and stained concrete. John had secretly bought the torch with some Christmas money his mother had not audited and this was the first time he had used it on a free adventure. The harsh brilliant stem of light made sharp shadows from the bramble tendrils that now grew out of every crack in the tarmac. The boarded-up entrance to the flats had long been vandalized and kicked in and from it the boys smelt the strong odour of damp and other strange unpleasant smells that breathe from dead and vandalized properties.

John made a violent kick at a pile of beer cans that had been left in the entrance and they rattled round the entrance hall like machine gun fire. Broken glass on the floor tinkled softly like distant alarm bells. The boys followed John warily across the hall, not liking the look of the wide open lift shafts. The lift doors and safety boarding had been smashed into the shaft. They looked like entrances to deep underground dungeons.

John made his way to the bottom of the stairs where a cold current of air made ancient leaves scratch the floor with a disturbing sound. For a few seconds John let the trunk of vivid torchlight rest on the rectangular caverns of the lift shafts. He gave a knowing and sinister chuckle that none of the boys knew how to respond to. Then he let the light rest on the walls that were nests of graffiti and sprayed tags. Perhaps John suddenly realized that some of the boys were reading messages he was unable to read for he abruptly aimed the light beam at the stairs.

'Come on. Follow me.' His voice was unusually low and vibrating with the excitement he felt. Had the boys been able to see his expression they would have been amazed at the change. He felt he was on the verge of all his ambitions and he trembled slightly with the tension. He felt free of home and school with all their criticisms and failures.

The stairs were climbed in scuffling hushed whispering. He stopped outside a door labelled '7a'. He recalled his father going in there and taking pictures to send to the MP and three newspapers. John pulled out the key from his pocket with a gesture rather like the gunman in his favourite video. He unlocked the door and stood in the entrance.

'This is it. This is where we come.' He was thinking of the teenage boys who delivered the papers and rode up and down the road enraging his parents with their shouts and noise. 'I can't let you in. My friends are older than me and it's their den.'

There was a long silence while John bathed in

daydreams and fantasies. The boys could smell the must and damp that softly blew around them from the flat. They heard something scratch and rattle that sounded horribly ratlike. John slowly surfaced from the comforting waters of his dreams and nodded at the boys in a superior way. He felt strong and in control. He'd never felt better. His feelings were soothed and his face relaxed. He locked and closed the door with a semicircle of admiring faces regarding him in respectful silence. Once more they scuffled down the stairs.

Only Adam heard him mutter, 'So watch out, Wilkinson. I've marked your card.'

Outside the moon was sharpened to stainless-steel lustre. The night had hardened into sharp shadows. The world had changed and the boys were silent and subdued. Only John was buoyant with power and triumph. The atmosphere of the flats had unnerved the boys. None of them had ever trusted John and to discover the rumours about his den and his friends were true alarmed them. They were all aware of things that John might do that before had only been shadowy fears and half formed rumours. They had a new respect and a fear of him. He was in with the older boys. He was tougher and harder than they had thought. Perhaps John sensed this for he suddenly tilted his head back and called out something the boys could not understand. But they sensed its meaning. It was the cry of someone who knows they can do what they like, when they like, and not let anyone get in their way.

Sam had left the house for the flats sometime earlier with Spot, lighter of heart than he had been for hours. The knowledge that John was out of the area gave him a sense of incredible well being, all the stronger because of the contrast of the earlier depression. He had binoculars round his neck, the ones he had persuaded his father to buy at a car boot sale on their camping holiday in Cornwall. Sam had told his father they were a fantastic bargain. They were 15×30 magnification, ideal for looking at the night sky. Sam had told his reluctant father it would be the best five pounds he had ever spent.

Sam walked onwards to the flats, eager for night and darkness, the binoculars swinging and bumping against his chest. The dog ran ahead excitedly. He liked walks with Sam best of all. Sam stood still for minutes and there was every chance to investigate every smell. Because he had eaten a good tea, Sam felt confident and was able to convince himself John was out of the way. John was making empty big-mouthed threats, he told himself. Sam even whistled softly as he entered the overgrown grounds. Unlike the other boys he was not scratched by brambles or stung by nettles. He knew his way around perfectly in the dark.

Sam arrived at the part of the flat grounds that had been intended as a playground and sports area. Although thistles and nettles were invading with every month that passed, it was still easy to walk across. He made his way to the middle where there was an unrestricted view of the sky over the nearby countryside. Here, one August evening, he had seen a shower of silver meteors. He wondered grimly if one had been the falling capsule that had hatched John, the cosmic cuckoo sent to capture Earthlings.

But then he let out a sigh of deep content as he gazed up into the deep blue of the sky. The first stars were blossoming and he quickly identified the great square of

Pegasus and then Andromeda. Andromeda was his favourite star group of this time of year. He raised his binoculars and focused them on the nebula, a spiral nebula, a far distant galaxy of stars. He sighed again. There, in the circle of his vision, was a galaxy of stars, perhaps with life and worlds, the light taking two million light years to reach him and then flash through the prisms of the binoculars, then into his eyes and brain. He stared through the lens wondering about strange forms of life and the fact he was looking at light that was now history.

He ignored the hoot of a tawny owl, because he knew the owl colony well. He took no notice of a loud shout because the teenagers were always round the flats on private and mysterious expeditions of their own. The owl was behind him, near to the hole in the long-abandoned ornamental rockery. Every spring the owls nested there and every spring Sam kept Spot away. Sam took these sounds as a natural and usual part of his evening walks with Spot.

Sam's attention was riveted on the spiral galaxy. He began to imagine a journey to it. He was convinced it would happen one day. He thought of himself zooming there at the speed of light, a distance of two million light years, then zooming back. If the Law of Relativity was correct then he would not have aged, but John would have long ago turned into a fossil. The thought of that made him smile into the skies until a shout, very close by, made him freeze in body and mind. He felt strength draining from him like matter sucked into a black hole. Happiness and the stars were sucked away. He knew with a chilling terror who that loud voice belonged to.

Sam swore at Spot who was wriggling backwards out of a rabbit hole like a rocket slowly emerging from a bunker—and making a lot of noise about it. Once launched Spot streaked towards the shout leaving a trail of very loud barks. Spot sensed that John's shout was that of a fellow animal out on the hunt. Spot had every intention of being in on the kill. And experience had told him that when humans made noises like this life became very interesting.

Sam swore again, this time with a hint of tears deep in his voice. He knew that when Spot was excited he forgot all his training and would jump up at people. He would even give a few harmless nips if he was wild enough. No way could Sam run away with his dog behaving like that. With a cold heavy sickness in his stomach, just like that of six hours earlier, Sam moved towards the voices and barking at the front of the flats. He knew John would make the most of being nipped by Spot, issuing more threats. Worse, he could imagine Mrs Snow ordering Spot to be 'put down'. These thoughts pushed him into the danger zone.

When he reached the former car park he could see Spot leaping wildly in the light beam of a powerful torch. He called Spot's name feebly but the dog did not respond. But John had recognized the dog—he had envied it for years—and was looking into the shadows for Sam. He could not believe his luck.

'Welcome to Cell Block 7a,' said John, unconsciously using his video speak voice. The other boys laughed loudly because it was John's party and Sam had not been invited. They did not, however, understand the signifi-cance of John's joke. There had been some sneers and jeers mixed with the laughter. They all knew Sam was the latest victim and self preservation on their part couldn't help keeping things that way. These feelings were strengthened by the pile of videos, tapes, discs, and games they had seen piled on the Snows' kitchen table. They knew these were to be the parting gifts for the guests. Sam was way out in an orbit of his own.

Then everyone turned at the sound of a powerful car making its way towards the flats, headlamps carving up the darkness, stereo system making the atmosphere quiver and the big engine supremely confident in its approach. It was John's father searching for his adopted son, sent out by Mrs Snow to return the exploring chick to the nest. The gold and blue coffee pots were empty and she had got what she wanted. The boys crowded round the splendid car as the engine stopped and the stereo died in the night.

Mr Snow climbed out. He never walked even the shortest distances, preferring his car to add status to his progress. All his exercise took place in a first class gym. He smiled down at the boys as though they were junior executives.

Mr Snow knew only work and his business. His own father had founded the Snow White Babywear firm. Mr Snow joined in wholeheartedly and extended the business. He had pioneered Snow White Super Disposable Nappies, Snow White Babymilk and a vast range of gleaming white wood cots and nursery furniture. He had worked so hard looking after, and profiting from, other people's babies he had had no time to marry and have any for himself. He had only been too delighted to marry the beautiful lawyer and find a ready-made son in John. Already he treated John like a junior partner.

He smiled broadly at the boys. His only strategy when faced with children was to arrange a competition and he did it now. 'Right then, lads. You, and you, and you, and you can ride in my new car. Wipe your shoes, lads.

78

Get in. We'll see who can be first back at the front door, John. And remember my motto in life, John. To be second is to be last.'

He swung himself into the soft leather of the driving seat and revved the engine with great roars and throaty heavings. The big car leapt into the night. John let out a matching growl and plunged into the undergrowth in a mad dash to defeat his father.

Mr Snow purred through the night, a look of great content on his face, talking at the boys in the car. 'Pretty soon this dump will be mine, so John and his friends will be free to roam on it when they choose. But don't come here till I've signed and ring-fenced it and got in the dogs. A place like this attracts all sorts of undesirables, drop-outs, layabouts . . . you know . . . But I'll soon sort it out. Building executive houses on it for my top men.' He swung the great car expertly out of the pocked and weed-filled drive on to the main road. Smoothly and powerfully the car reached maximum allowed speed and Mr Snow, smiling faintly, watched the road.

Sam, the outsider, remained on the edge of the night and the activity. Spot returned to his side with tail depressed, sad he had not been told to join the race. He had liked the look of the boys diving under a distant hedge. Peering into the gloom Sam was surprised to see Adam fiddling with his trainers. His shoe had come off when it caught in a dislodged paving slab. For a moment, as long as it takes a shooting star to cross the heavens, Sam had the hope that Adam had stayed behind to ask him to walk home with him. But there was no hope. Adam had been captured by the leisure centre, the party, the gifts, and the car. Adam was now aware that Sam was no longer an acceptable friend. He could not cope with being alone with Sam. It made words pour out of him.

'It's really wicked in there. Excellent den. He's got a great place. Nobody would know you were there for days and days.'

Sam found Adam had gone, rushing to join the race, eager for the CD he had spotted. Sam was alone with the moon and the spiral nebula, the frosty air, and the tawny owl. Distant shouts in the direction of the security lights' glare told him that somebody had won. And, like him, somebody had lost.

NINE

The next morning, the morning after the party, Friday, John entered the classroom with a definite swagger and a smile far from pleasant. Under his arm was a plastic bottle of Coke and a sliced white loaf. He managed to give Sam a sly nudge as he passed his table by the door.

'Prison rations,' said John as Sam looked up startled. And afraid.

Sam had managed to get himself to school—just. Two thoughts had given him a raft to float hopes on. The first was the fact that the weekend approached. Sam knew that John was expensively entertained at weekends with trips to theme parks, sporting events, leisure centres, and everything money could buy. John would be with his parents all the time and could not possibly take anyone prisoner. The other hope was the consideration that if John had meant to take him prisoner, he would have done so the previous evening. And yet the raft was rocked by a storm of doubts. Sam suspected that the arrival of John's father had stopped something very nasty from happening. There was a growing wildness in John that made Sam fear that even the weekend could not prevent John from planning something terrible.

Sam watched John go to the trays. He suddenly felt there was no point in being. Mrs Firth was frowning at some record sheets of the children's and for half an hour failed to see there were two boys in the class who did not read a word. She had, however, noted the bottle and cheap loaf on John's table but she had decided to say nothing. She decided that a skirmish over such trivia was not wise. In any case she had a tired headache and could not face a battle with John over groceries.

John remained in his seat turning the plastic bottle round and round and patting the loaf every time Sam glanced in his direction, on average every fifty seconds. After fifteen minutes John left his seat and pretended to look at a display of books near to Sam's table.

'It costs money buying in for a prisoner,' he said quietly.

John's mother had left him at the school gates as usual. There had been a quick jewelled perfumed peck of a kiss and a 'Bye bye, my chicken,' then the car had whispered away. John watched her disappear then he had rushed across to the local shop. It was a novelty for John to enter an ordinary shop. His mother gathered food for him on her slickly organized weekly shopping trips to the supermarkets. She saw no point in dragging a bored John to the supermarket. She flitted quickly around the food bays listening to parents arguing with children over food and sweets and seeing the pained looks on children's faces. She congratulated herself that her organization meant John did not have to suffer such tedium. Apart from sports shops, computer stores, and record shops John visited no other shops.

When John was four Mrs Snow had taken him with her to her favourite high class department store. In five minutes John had lifted the frocks of models to discover what lay beneath, spat out a low fat fruit bar into two plastic legs displaying superior tights, and opened a till to measure the financial success of the store.

John had no idea of the price of food. He had taken a pound coin to the shop confident that this would be enough to enable him to buy food for his den. He had wanted bacon, eggs, Cup-a-Soups, and salami—all frowned upon at home. Had he not had a spare fifty pence in his jacket there would only have been enough for a drink. Surprised and angry, John had decided to buy food just to tease Sam. He would return later and secretly buy what he needed for the den and his prisoner.

It was a pleasant autumnal morning and Mrs Firth thought she would take the PE lesson outdoors. Looking at the endless paperwork had made her headache worse. She also wanted to take the children outside again and make them behave properly. Today there would be no arguments and quarrels, just simple kicking, passing, and throwing skills. At the end of the lesson her headache had cleared and she congratulated herself that the class had behaved perfectly and John had not 'showed off' once. She had not seen everything.

She had led the children from the front, leading them outside into the fresh air. John had positioned himself near Sam, almost at the back of the line. Sam was wearing a pair of shorts handed down from his brother and faded by much washing. His trainers had cost £7.99 from a market stall. John was resplendent in the latest kit of Manchester United (a team admired by Mr Snow) bought new the last weekend. His trainers had cost £59.99. He gave Sam a slight push as they walked along and Sam had swerved.

'Look where you're going, jumble sale,' said John. There had been a rustle of laughter. 'Even his knickers are bought from a market stall,' John said to Adam. Mr Snow's and John's crisp white boxer shorts, embroidered initials on the front, were bought in London.

But the nastiest attack had come when they had been dribbling footballs round yellow cones.

'Watch yourself, gaolbird,' John had remarked pleasantly as Sam moved in front of John in the line. The mention of prisons disquieted Sam more than anything.

Playtime now found Sam totally ignored by the other boys in the class. This was the worst part of his new life. The girls, well aware of what was going on, but scared of John, kept well out of the situation. Caroline and Jenny discussed it as they ate their apples. Caroline had always liked Sam. Yet each time they looked in Sam's direction they matched it with an anxious glance in John's direction. It was easy to pick out Sam, he was on his own. It was also easy to glimpse John's cubelike mass in the middle of an admiring crowd.

After break Mrs Firth took them to the video room where she intended they would learn more about cuckoos. Automatically Sam now went and sat in the space at the front that nobody else wanted. He watched, the back of his neck already hurting, as Mrs Firth inserted the tape. He stared at the teacher blank faced and unhappy.

'Settle down everybody. Sam, do try to look interested even though you clearly can't be bothered this morning. Jack, I shall pretend that I have not seen the Cyberpet you have brought into the room. You know Mrs Highfield does not like you to bring them to school. If I see it just *once* I shall send you to her and say that it is interfering with your work. And Adam, I do hope that *silly* grin is going to leave your face. Pardon? Yes, I'm sure John tells wonderful jokes *but I am waiting to begin.*' The class, hearing her voice rise in volume, became silent. They dutifully stared at the video and prepared to be bored.

Obediently they watched the meadow pipits feed the

chick that had been put in their nest by the mother cuckoo. In a state of dull attention they watched the chick take morsels of food. Then indifference and boredom changed to dismay and horror. They saw the chick, when the pipits had gone, suddenly lever itself under a pipit's egg and wriggle till it balanced the egg on a hollow on its back. Then, crawling in a reptilian way to the nest side, the chick heaved and the egg fell from the nest. After another feed from the foster parents the chick disposed of the remaining eggs.

'Mrs Firth, that's cruel,' cried Caroline. There was a chorus of agreement. Many in the class felt it was vicious and savage the way the chick disposed of the pipit's eggs.

'I'm afraid Nature can be very cruel,' said Mrs Firth, pressing the Pause button as the cuckoo made its final ascent. 'Nature often allows the strongest and the fittest to survive, Caroline, and the weaker creatures are left to . . . er . . . die.'

'My dad says life is like that anyway,' said John in a very loud voice. 'The weak always go under.' He gave a strange all-knowing smile to Sam who had turned round to look and listen.

Mrs Firth appeared uncomfortable. She was pleased that John was joining in the discussion but she disliked what she heard. Once she had listened to John's father at a Parents' Evening insist that the school must rubbish all the other nearby schools if it were to come out best. She glanced anxiously at her notes and tried to steer the talk back to the National Curriculum.

'The cuckoo is trying to get rid of the other birds so he can spread his own cuckoo genes around,' announced Mrs Firth reading from the video booklet. Several of the class gazed at her in wonder, thinking of tiny blue-denim, drinking-straw-thin jeans that the tiny cuckoo perhaps wore on its legs. 'The cuckoo is doing what its genes are telling it to do,' continued Mrs Firth. (Three children's mouths became O's of astonishment.) 'It's not like human bullying or killing in wars,' she said lamely, 'even though it looks like it.'

Mrs Firth found it suddenly impossible to simplify animal and human behaviour. She cleared her throat importantly and tried again. 'The world is full of creatures all wanting food and space for their own kind. And yes, humans seem to do this too . . .' She gave up. Tried once more. 'I suppose we're all like the cuckoos in a way.'

She switched the video back on and was intensely relieved to see the camera had briefly focused on a nice humble bee going into a nice bluebell growing close by the smashed remains of the pipit eggs. The bee and the bluebell looked pretty and easy to understand.

The destruction of the eggs and the mention of bullying distressed Sam. So had John's ugly smile. A surge of sickness entered his stomach followed by an instinctive need to leave the room and run for his life. In its turn this was followed by a sensation of helpless weakness. He felt the will to live ebb from him. This he found worrying and for the next few minutes he worried as much about these new feelings as he did over John's bullying.

So the day dragged onwards. Sam was absorbed in himself and no longer cared that nobody was talking to him. He was even thankful that John did not make any more threats. And it was a Friday after all. If he could just make it to hometime, that would be something . . .

There was the usual mega tidy up at three o'clock because it was Friday and Sam was extra careful to avoid contact with John in the bustle of it all. He was relieved to hear Mrs Firth hustle everyone back to their places earlier than was usual on Friday.

'Listen very carefully. That includes you, Harry. I don't care if there are ninety-nine wasps in the window, this is far more important, so *listen*. Before you all dash off home I want you to spend fifteen minutes with your spelling books. I'm going to give you a spelling test on Monday morning. I shall discuss the results with your parents on open evening.'

Whiteness flushed into John's face with the speed of bleach turning dirty washing white. Finally his face was the colour of the white marble in his mother's super-kitchen. Mrs Firth did not notice this dramatic colour change.

'Get your spelling books with the lists of words I've given you. Copy out the word. Cover it up and try to write the word correctly. I don't care *where* the wasp has gone, or is going, Harry. Then uncover the spelling and see if you got it right. If you got it correct do the same with the next word. If you got it wrong keep repeating the process till you get it right. If it's gone inside your spelling book you must have let it in, Harry. Pardon? Of course you can do your spellings. Go to the window and shake it out carefully. *Sit down, Emma*. It does *not* need two of you.'

John got the first spelling he attempted hopelessly wrong. He tried again but the letters would not fall into order. He could not understand why some letters stuck together like 'ck' or 'ea'. He was bewildered. He began to see his mother's frowning face on the paper as she saw the low mark of the spelling test. Panic made John suddenly stand up. Last year, the years before that, he would have thrown a wobbly. Now he did have a little more control over himself. Nevertheless he needed to do something to make himself feel better. He walked over to Sam. Mrs Firth was looking at last year's results and silently praying the children had improved.

Sam was happier than he had been all day. The day, the week, was nearly over. The class had been silenced and it did not show up that nobody was speaking to him. Moreover he was quite happy to do the spellings. Without seemingly trying, spellings always came right for him. John watched him silently and ferociously for a few seconds, watching him get each spelling correct. He made a swoop for Sam's rubber.

'Can I borrow your rubber? Thanks.'

John took Sam's rubber back to his place and began a frantic rubbing out of his own smudged and scruffy spellings. Sam decided to say nothing. Having your rubber pinched was considerably more acceptable than threatened imprisonment. John rubbed so hard with Sam's rubber that it made a hole in the page. Rage and fear gripped John. He broke Sam's rubber in two, crumbled it in his fists to fragments, then crossed the room and threw the crumbs over Sam's spellings.

Concentrating on the spellings had thawed Sam's mind out of its frozen fear-chilled state. He was no longer the passive Sam he had been for all of that Friday. He reacted in the way he would have done before the Big Threat. He called out.

'Mrs Firth, John's broken up my rubber deliberately.'

Sam's angry voice was as loud as John's. The class all looked up eager to abandon their struggle with words to watch the start of a more interesting battle. Mrs Firth felt her spirits sink. This was the sort of confrontation with John she dreaded. Sighing, she prepared for showdown and meltdown. She need not have worried.

John was greatly worried over the tests. He was planning an escape to the flats before the test, but in the meantime the last thing he wanted was a letter home. He knew the first thing his mother would ask was, 'And what was the lesson you were having, darling, when you lost your temper?' This would be followed by an immediate visit to school with the question, 'Is John having problems with his spellings?' Then she would want to see his spelling book and the balloon would go up. John spoke loudly.

'Very sorry, Sam. I just bent it like you do and it fell to bits. It's because it was a cheapo rubber.' John spread his hands out as if to demonstrate the nature of cheap rubbers and clear himself of blame. 'They're probably only ten pence from the post office. I'll bring twenty pence on Monday so he can buy a new one. He can keep the change for good will.'

Mrs Firth sagged with relief. She felt unable to cope with John's brand of bother at the end of a busy and tiring week. She was exhausted and could not have faced a meeting with Mrs Snow after school. She cleared her throat loudly to restore her authority.

'Well, that's sorted. Which reminds me. Please bring your own rubber for Monday for the big test. Spelling tests are difficult and I had rather you rub out than cross out. Sometimes children alter the word so much I cannot see whether it is right or wrong. A rubber is a good thing to have by you. Yes, Laura? No, you may *not* bring Tipp-Ex. It is not allowed. I don't care, Laura, if your mother could get everyone a free bottle from her office storeroom. So don't forget. A rubber first thing on Monday. Now, put your things away and off you go and have a great weekend.'

Sam was drenched with overwhelming fury. He

needed a rubber for Monday and his had been destroyed. He would not touch John's money. Not ever. And he had no pocket money left. Not a single one pence. He had spent his last two pounds on a magazine about astronomy. He was certain there was no extra money at home. Every penny was accounted for at his house. He fixed Mrs Firth with a poisonous snake stare which she pretended not to see. He fixed his glare to John who was white and thoughtful and tidying his tray. Sam snapped and shouted across the classroom.

'If you won't do anything about my rubber then I will. My rubber's been deliberately bust and I'm going to report it to Mrs Highfield and I want something doing about *him*.'

Sam slammed out of the room, leaving the class, Mrs Firth, and John in astonished silence.

TEN

Mrs Highfield felt like a cushion being stuffed with happenings. The afternoon had been so very busy. She was breathless with it all, rose pink with dashing about, her face matched the pink of her dress and earrings. She felt her brain could not take in anything else. She had shown two ultra-critical parents round the school who were thinking, but only thinking, of sending their child to the school. They had asked two hundred questions—or so it seemed. Then she had been on her knees in the playground peering down a small drain that contained the water meter. The Governors, which really meant Mrs Snow, wanted to know exactly how much water the children drank, flushed away, or wasted every day. The curtain rail in the hall fell down at half-past two and smothered three infants who had to be loved and pacified. The mum and dad who helped in the library had found an expensive encyclopaedia was missing. The nurse had come to discuss the talk on sex education she was to give on Monday and she had to be given coffee and chocolate wheaten biscuits. Then the vicar came to discuss the harvest festival and he liked tea and bourbon biscuits; William in reception had stabbed Lois with scissors; the telephone was not working; cook called in to say someone had eaten a dinner who had not paid; and Mrs Richardson had banged her head and needed aspirin and ten minutes of sympathy. The cushion of her brain felt about to burst any minute, and, now, oh dear, whatever did Sam want?

'I'm being bullied.'

'Oh, Sam, are you sure? That is a very serious accusation, you know. Think carefully back to that big project the whole school did on bullying last term. We all agreed that we would have no bullying in our school, it was quite unacceptable, we all decided, do you remember, dear?' She paused for breath, breathless once more with another problem. 'Do you remember that wonderful school booklet we all made with the promise in it everyone would stop bullying?'

Sam opened his mouth to say he was being bullied whether there was a school booklet or not, but somehow the words would not come out. Mrs Highfield seemed to smother him with a feathery barrier. Her mouth had become an O of sorrow, disbelief, disapproval and she was already looking on her shelves for the booklet. Sam briefly wondered at the power of teachers to stifle speech, control the mind, prevent you saying what was really the matter. Mrs Highfield grasped two books with a smile. Sam stared at her dumbly. Her room was a bit like the office of a shop with big files about money and lots of coloured books and brochures. All the books were full of facts and answers but not solutions.

Mrs Highfield handed Sam the booklets with a relieved smile. Thank goodness they had spent weeks and weeks on a bullying project. At least this problem did not need any complicated decisions, any long-term planning. It had been done. Her coral pink lips relaxed into a smile. Her brain did not feel so tightly packed now.

Sam stared helplessly. One book was a pillar box red and proudly announced OUR SCHOOL'S ANTI-BULLYING POLICY. The other booklet was titled MAKING FRIENDS AT CROSSROADS PRIMARY SCHOOL. This booklet had a sickly green cover and revealed a picture on the cover of John and Mr Snow

92

at the tombola stall at the school's summer fayre. They had just won a prize and were in a circle of admiring parents. Mr Snow had paid for the expensive printing of the book.

'Remember, Sam? All the work we did together? All the activities with each other? The meetings with mums and dads? Yes, I'm sure you do. See. It says here—and you helped to make these rules, Sam—"If you are being bullied first talk to your teacher or a grown-up in private". Now, have you done that? I'm sure Mrs Firth would listen to all you have to say.' Mrs Highfield felt the problem was solved.

Sam's personal universe entered what he later called his Big Bang. It was the birth of a new universe, a new Sam. It was a singularity, as one of his books called it. A spinning nebula of red and black whirled and rotated in front of his eyes. It eclipsed Mrs Highfield and in the whirlwind he did not hear the bad words he shouted at her. At first there was a hole in the vortex through which Sam saw parts of the room, John's stupid face on the booklet, a graph showing finance, a crack in the ceiling. Then there was nothing but elemental rage that shook him with thunderous violence. Finally, he heard himself shouting in a strange new silent world. 'I am being bullied, I tell you. He's calling me names. He's making fun of my clothes. He says he's going to lock me up. Why don't you listen?' Then he was aware he was on the floor with a circle of adults, like circling planets, moving silently round him. It had become very quiet.

He was taken home in Mrs Davidson's car. Her lips, redder than Mrs Highfield's, were a thin line of disapproval. She thought he should be excluded for shouting such terrible things at the headteacher. Sam held a letter from Mrs Highfield to his parents. When they reached the house Mrs Davidson snatched the letter from Sam and gave it personally to the astonished Mrs Wilkinson. She did not trust Sam, she made that very plain to see.

Sam followed his mother into the house and saw with dismay that his grandfather was there. Sam and his grandfather were great friends and he wanted to keep the letter about the Big Bang from him. To add to his misery he saw everyone gathered round for family tea. Friday teatime was always a family festival, with plans for the weekend being discussed and sometimes special treats on the table.

Sam's grandfather was blind. Like his own story of his life, Sam on good days thought his grandfather's story had a happy ending. He had been a fireman fighting a huge blaze in a factory, rescuing people, when a container of chemicals had exploded. Several people had been killed. Sam's grandfather had been badly injured, but he recovered. His eyes had not. He had been given a medal and a large sum of compensation money. Now he had a guide dog called Lenny and on happy days Sam accepted all this easily.

Sam looked bleakly at the family, with his mother behind him. Lenny stared up at him from under the table, softly thumping his tail on the floor. Spot, greatly in awe of Lenny who smelt like a dog but did not behave like one (he made no attempt to exchange bottom-sniffing rituals), was in his basket. Spot's head was now the only moving thing in the room as he looked from Sam to Lenny and back again.

The envelope began to crackle and rip the silence as Mrs Wilkinson started to open it. Sam did not want this to happen, he wanted to shield his grandfather from the pain of the last few days. He had only happy times with his grandfather and he did not want to pollute this with misery. Like last Christmas after a very late Christmas tea. Sam had taken his grandfather and Lenny over to the flats. Lenny had steered the old man through the bushes and brambles with skilled ease. Spot had followed in subdued reverence. Then Sam had explained the winter stars. He had described the Pleiades like sparkling glittering pepper on a black plate. He had told him of great Sirius, winking huge and majestic like a blue ambulance light. Above Sirius there had been Orion, the three stars of his belt resting on some invisible tilted ruler. Then he had told him of Taurus the Bull, with its red eye of the star Aldebaran, a red and angry bull's eye. His grandfather told him he had never had such a happy Christmas night. Now Sam heard his grandfather talk to his mother.

'What is it, Barbara? You're opening a letter?'

'Yes, I know I am, Dad. It's from Sam's headteacher.'

'Read it to us then.'

For a second or two Sam's mother hesitated. Then with a shrug she read it aloud.

'Dear Mr and Mrs Wilkinson. I am sending Sam home with Mrs Davidson, our child care assistant, after a serious loss of Sam's self control. He seems to have strangely over-reacted to some trivial classroom mischief by another boy, in which Sam's rubber was broken into fragments. The boy in question promptly offered to pay for a new rubber.

Sam seems to think this is a case of serious bullying. I have had a long talk to Sam's class teacher, Mrs Firth, and we are both convinced that Sam has no cause to think he is being bullied.

We have a firm anti-bullying policy in our school which the children, parents, and teachers all worked together to make. Perhaps you will both recall the happy atmosphere of the evenings we spent together, during last term, when we were formulating our anti-bullying strategies. I am sure that when Sam has regained his composure he will agree that he was not being bullied in our school.

Sam is the first pupil to complain of bullying since we completed the project. May I repeat we feel Sam has no cause to worry. Mrs Firth and I will be delighted to talk to you both about this incident at any time convenient to you if you wish to see us. Please do not hesitate to call us if you have any worries or concerns, we will be only too pleased to help.

Yours sincerely, Nancy Highfield, Headteacher.'

There was a silence in the room. Nobody was sure how to respond. Sam saw his grandfather's hand move over the table like a friendly crab, seeking his own hand. But Sam was afloat on a sea of chill misery and could not touch it. His grandfather spoke to him.

'What's up, Sam?'

Sam did his best to explain to the waiting room and to his bewildered parents. Sam had never had trouble with school before this. The more Sam tried to explain to everybody the more it sounded as if the letter was reasonable and true. 'He's always calling me names, saying things about my clothes and shoes.' Sam stopped. Then blurted out the truth that so scared him. 'He says he's going to lock me up.'

There was laughter round the table for the first time since Sam had arrived home late. 'That's a laugh,' said Sam's dad. 'If anyone's locked up it's Mrs Snow's precious son John. And he probably knows he's a prisoner in his own home. That's why he's threatening you with it.' It was a shrewd remark and comforted Sam a fraction.

'He just got my rubber and . . . just smashed it.' Sam was very close to breaking down.

'He's paying you for it, isn't he?' asked Richard, Sam's middle brother, his mouth stuffed full of chocolate walnut cake. One of the pleasures of the usual Friday tea was that Sam's grandfather supplied the family with treats they could not often afford. 'And if he doesn't, then break his neck, the great, ugly, fat worm.'

Sam said nothing. It was all right for Richard, he thought. He was already six feet tall, tall and strong for his age. Nobody had ever bullied Richard. Sam wondered if he understood what the word meant.

'And is that all this is about?' said Sam's mother. She had been at work since eight o'clock and her mood was as worn out as her body. It made her miss the point of everything. 'If you think that by saying John is making fun of that jacket you'll get another one, you can think again, young man. We've not got the money to buy you clothes to please John Snow.' She folded the letter with quick movements that showed she had had her fill of problems for that day. The letter was put on a pile at the end of the kitchen table. Then there was a long, long silence again.

After a minute Sam stood up and looked round the table accusingly. He had not eaten anything. He felt cheated, let down, isolated. The stories about his being dumped on the hospital steps and his grandfather's blindness seemed to be two of the world's greatest tragedies at that moment. The broken rubber grew to be one of the most important facts in the world. He wanted to do the test well on Monday, tests seemed important to grown-ups. He left the room without speaking.

On the stairs he heard his grandfather say something to Richard and Richard's voice explaining something. His grandfather got more words out of Richard in five minutes than the rest of the family did in a year. Sam failed to see that his grandfather was allowing Sam space and time to recover and was trying to bring back some warmth to the family gathering. Instead he felt jealous of Richard and he imagined Richard stuffing the delicious cakes. Having no tea inside him made Sam more obsessive about the rubber than ever. He felt, too, that the family needed punishing for not sympathizing about his troubles with John.

Sam stood at the top of the stairs with all these feelings washing over him like a dark and troubled sea on a new hostile planet. Finally he went into Richard's room and took the large and very costly rubber that Richard had bought from the art shop in town for his GCSE Art work. He was some time in finding it amongst the homework, beakers, discs, and cans. All the time he could hear Richard talking and laughing below.

Feeling he had tried to solve one problem Sam went into his own room and attempted to read a space magazine. But he kept looking in the direction of John's house with its one tall watching chimney stack over the trees. Sam had the horrible feeling there was somebody watching and waiting over there.

ELEVEN

John saw his father on Monday morning, the day of the test. That was unusual for a Monday morning. Mr Snow sat at the breakfast bar, mingling the fragrance of aftershave with Blue Mountain coffee. A large breakfast cup steamed by his side and he was frowning at a laptop computer. A silver spoon was aggressively upright in a jar of black cherry jam.

''Morning, son. Anything special today? Games? Tests?'

'Yes,' said John in a small voice strangled and choked with despair at what lay ahead. For once John was too disturbed to lie.

'Be sure you come out on top, son. It's the only way in this life. Don't let anyone stand in your way, get in the way of the sun. Go for it. Life's for the taking and if you don't take what's on offer somebody else will.'

Both Mr and Mrs Snow were unaware of John's rising panic. Mr Snow softly rattled the computer keys and Mrs Snow wrote instructions with a gold fountain pen. She was writing a note to the cleaning lady who came to tidy the weekend away. John could feel his stomach heaving as he pushed his low fat cereal round the blue and gold cereal bowl. He wanted to run. Hide in the flats. But he knew the escape to the flats needed another day of planning at least and there was Wilkinson to think of.

His stomach churned at the thought of Sam. He hated and envied him. He knew he would come out top. Sam Wilkinson was always standing in his way. Both Mr and Mrs Snow would have been amazed at their son's unhappiness. They thought they were giving him the very best start in life. John excused himself and left the kitchen. He would take the key to the flats. John had had enough of the day already.

His mother watched him through the steam of the delicious coffee. She felt content with her life, her kitchen, and all she was now able to give her son. Sunshine wrapped the kitchen with a golden contentment.

In the classroom there was a chill atmosphere of depressed expectation. The test hung in the air like a poisonous cloud. A few children who thought they might do well collected their books with ordinary speed. The rest moved slowly and a few, including John, were on the verge of stopping all purposeful movement, they were so overcome with the threat.

Mrs Firth was at her desk with a bright and strained Monday morning smile upon her face. Sam was in his place turning the pages of a book listlessly. Suddenly there was a bang in the cold room as John thumped down a pound coin on Sam's table. Everyone jumped. Nerves were bad that morning.

'Here's the money for the rubber. Keep the change and buy something for yourself.' Unconsciously John imitated the tone of his father giving a homeless man some cash for a cup of tea. With his back to Mrs Firth John dangled the key to the flats in front of Sam's nose. Sam pushed the pound coin away with contempt, but his hand shook as he did so. The key frightened him badly.

Mrs Firth's cheery smile vanished. John's behaviour was most inappropriate. But she had no time to explain or risk a floor show. The test had been set for all the Year Six children in the school and they all had to begin at the same time. So that was that. But she said in a very cold voice, 'Thank you, John. Ten pence was all you needed to replace the rubber you broke. Now sit down while I do the register.'

The test was administered like bitter medicine. Sweat masked John's face like a coating of clingfilm. Every single spelling went wrong. He almost cried with frustration. During the test desperation swelled to panic. His paper was a scuffed and unsavoury smudge of dreary mistakes. Looking over to Sam he noted Wilkinson writing words without any bother.

'These last few words please do not worry about,' said Mrs Firth. 'Only a few of you will be able to tackle them. Just don't try if you can't cope. It's the first forty words that are important. They will give us . . . er, you . . . the marks necessary.'

John gave a low soft moan. He doubted even if he had the first three right. He watched Sam with smouldering aggression and jealousy as Sam wrote the last word 'encyclopaedia' without any hesitation. Sam did not even use a rubber to try the word out once or twice.

'Yes. Well, that wasn't too bad, was it?' said Mrs Firth brightly, switching on a forced cheerful smile. 'Just take a breather, a little break.'

John was over at Sam's table almost before the words were out of her mouth. He clawed at Richard's rubber that Sam had brought for the test.

'You might come out top in spelling but you don't in rubbers or freedom,' snarled John with venomous energy. This vicious attack was hidden by the buzz of released tension in the classroom. But Sam shouted above the racket so that Mrs Firth would hear at once.

'Mrs Firth, John's got my rubber.'

Mrs Firth exploded loudly with a quick detonation. *'Oh, for goodness' sake.* What is the matter with this class? I have never before seen such a class that is so . . . so petty minded . . . and *so childish.* You are like a lot of silly infants. Sit down, Sam. *I said sit down.* If John has taken your rubber again take the pound coin and buy two. Though why you had to go over and touch it in the first place, John, I am at a loss to understand.' She lost her temper and lashed out at John. 'You are little better than some big greedy baby, John, passing another baby's pram and shooting out your mittens to snatch another baby's dummy or rattle.'

The class laughed at John, a little uncertainly, but they laughed. The memory of the party was fading. Both the class and Mrs Firth now expected a roll-around under the classroom tables accompanied by grunts and roars of anger. Instead, John remained quiet but with murder in his eyes and heart. As on Friday, he realized the test was a big enough problem without adding to it with bad behaviour. John's eyes gleamed and Sam saw his clasped hand gripping the key to the flats.

'Grow up, both of you,' continued Mrs Firth. 'All the important things there are in this life—' The class switched off now the comedy had vanished from her lecture. Some thought of the snack they were going to eat at break. Some thought about their plans for after school. Only John and Sam did not switch attention from each other.

' . . . and you had all better read in perfect silence with nobody saying a word, nobody leaving their place, *or touching other people's things.* I hope I make myself perfectly clear?' She gave John a meaningful stare. 'And that is aimed in your direction, John Snow.'

The class almost gasped. Surely John would fall to the floor after such a direct thrust. But John did not respond. He stared at *Easter Story* his mind swarming with evil plans. The class became deadly still. Experience told them someone would suffer after such a direct attack, if not sooner, then later.

Mrs Firth spent the rest of the morning teaching number skills. This consisted of table practice and endless columns of the four rules of number. Sam found it mind numbing. A few children liked it and John was one of them. Plain straight number work without words he found very soothing. Numbers behaved for him in a way words did not. He could organize numbers and make them do his bidding. John was pacified, just a little. In the afternoon they learned about how birds feed and they were taken to the video room to see how the baby cuckoo was fed.

The foster parents of the cuckoo did not appear to see there was anything wrong or threatening about their foster chick. The cuckoo slowly swelled and filled the delicate and beautiful nest. The chick was plump with greed and self-centred aggression. The parent pipits worked so hard they did not see anything wrong. After some time had passed the swollen chick made an attempt to leave the nest. It broke through the nest and waddled a few unlovely strides. It flapped its wings for the first time.

A blackbird spotted the strange chick and sensed there was something dangerous. The blackbird sounded its alarm call and made a move towards the chick as if an attempt to sort it out was to begin. But the chick opened its bill and made a reptile hissing, its big bill wide open. The blackbird moved away, still warning the other birds. None of them took any notice. They were all too busy gathering food and sorting out their own nests. The cuckoo continued to inflate.

At hometime Sam sped home after sneaking out in the confusion of putting everything away. He arrived home breathless and pale and slumped in front of the television while his father prepared the tea. His father was in a distant and quiet mood. His redundancy worried him greatly and he was lost in a maze of problems about bills, money, and credit cards. He hardly noticed Sam come in that day, least of all he did not notice Sam's pale and worried face. He certainly did not think it was strange that Sam was in front of the television instead of playing out, as he used to do before tea.

The television was the only sound in the kitchen. Sam's mum was at work and Richard was at rugby practice. When tea was ready it was eaten in silence, both Sam and his dad lost in their own anxieties. After the meal Sam's dad peered hopelessly at the jobs page in the paper and Sam slowly climbed the stairs to his room. He stayed there for an hour or more until he heard Richard and his mother arrive home together. He wandered aimlessly out on to the landing as Richard crashed up the stairs.

'You've been in my room.'

'I haven't.'

'Liar. You've taken my rubber. I saw it had gone this morning. You've taken my rubber because you can't stand up to that nerd Snow. Right.' Richard advanced. 'Give it back.'

'I've not got your rubber. It's probably lost in that

dustbin you call a desk under all those empty cans and magazines—'

'How did you know I kept it there if you haven't been in the room to look? OK, I want it back. I've said that to you once already.'

Richard grabbed Sam and pinned him against the wall of the landing. Richard was tired and very hungry after his practice, and was not pleased that his mother had insisted he took a shower before he had his tea. Sam jerked back against the wall, banged his head, gave a loud yelp of pain. Their mother appeared from the kitchen below, her strained white face peering up through the banisters and the gloom.

'Get in that shower, Richard. Now. Never mind why. Now. Go on. All this fuss over rubbers. First Sam at school and now you. And as for you, Sam, I don't know what's the matter, I really don't. We get a letter from school about your bad behaviour, and all that was about was a rubber. Now you're at it again. It's a pity you've nothing else to worry about except coats and rubbers. If you had had the sort of day I'd had at work you wouldn't be worrying over what make your coat is, or who's touched your rubber . . . ' She ran out of breath. She felt better after the eruption of her feelings and made her way back to the kitchen to drink some hot tea. But now it was Sam's turn to blow.

'Who said anything about coats? I thought this was about Richard and rubbers.'

'Don't start, Sam. Don't start. I've had enough. Just find Richard's rubber while he's in the shower.'

'Don't start, Sam. Don't start. Just find Richard's rubber,' mimicked Richard's muffled and steamy voice from behind the bathroom door. Then in his own voice, 'I'll kill you if you don't.'

Sam stamped and clumped down the stairs making a china jug on the telephone table jump and vibrate in sympathy to his angry steps. Sam began to shout in the same way he shouted to Mrs Firth.

'I'll find his bloody rubber. But if I don't come back remember it was all over one bloody rubber. Oh, and a coat. We mustn't forget the coat.'

Sam went to the front door, opened it with much rattling, then slammed it with gusto. He ran down the front path. He was greatly disturbed by everything, at odds with everybody and no longer thought rationally. The Big Bang with Mrs Highfield had brought about a new cosmos. He was in a different world, he still did not know his way about or what to feel about things. Not thinking coherently, he ran out of the gate into the gathering darkness, uncaring about where he was going, just intent on running away.

'If I were to cease to exist nobody would care,' he muttered as he ran down the lamplit street.

Back in the house Sam's father looked up for the first time from the jobs supplement. His face looked strangled with worry and tension. 'I'll go after him,' he said in a flat voice. 'It's getting dark.'

'Just let him cool off,' said his wife. After giving vent to her feelings she was relaxing on the settee with a cup of tea and another sandwich. Through the fog of weariness she had dimly sensed that Sam needed to be left alone by Richard and she had ordered him into the shower. Now she also guessed that Sam needed time and space to cool down. She thought he would be in the garden and she fully expected him to creep back silently for the dog and go off and stare at his precious stars. She gave a sigh and wriggled her toes to the warmth of the gas fire.

'Let him simmer down. It's a stage they all go through. They get all clever and think they know it all. That one in the shower was just the same at Sam's age. Trying to dictate what he should eat and wear. It's part of growing up. Give him twenty minutes by himself.'

'It's getting dark. And he's not got the dog—'

'Leave him, I said. He'll not thank you for going to him straight away. You're finding problems before they exist.'

Sam's dad heard the rising note in his wife's voice and did not want to start a row. He kept quiet as she shouted up to Richard.

'Hurry out of that shower. It all costs money. There's a sandwich, salad, and a jacket potato down here if you can be bothered to come downstairs for it. Then you can take the dog and make it up with Sam.'

There was no reply from the bathroom. Mrs Wilkinson stretched out in the warmth, switched the television to *Coronation Street* and blissfully escaped into a world where problems were no longer hers but were fun to watch.

Sam jogged quickly away from home. He did not care if he never returned. The new universe had no pleasure in it. He noticed the wind parting the clouds, saw a dashing half moon rushing along with him, saw Saturn rest on the rim of a cloud but they were all seen without pleasure. Like Sam's mind the night was full of emptiness, pools of dark between the street lamps, lakes of nothingness between moonlit clouds. He ran along the road, blown by the wind, pulled by the moon, accompanied by the first leaves of autumn scuttling round his feet. He had no real purpose, no feelings—just the need to escape from everything.

The running made him breathless and he found

himself in the large bus shelter opposite the school. He flopped down on the hard seat and let his breathing return to normal. The night moved around him. The moon sailed in the cloud islands, the leaves rustled, the wind ruffled his hair. He felt very alone and this brought him to his feet after a time. He moved to the entrance of the shelter and almost fell as his foot slipped on an empty can concealed in the pile of blown leaves. Sam lashed out at the can and kicked it over the road where it landed with a rattle. He searched out three more and kicked those over the road, the last narrowly missing a passing car. He was not certain why he did this. It was something to do in a world that no longer pleased him.

When there were no more cans left he aimlessly walked out of the shelter and disinterestedly saw there was a light in the school and the main door was open. He expected that the cleaners were completing one of their mysterious tasks. Like a shooting star across an empty sky came the thought—why should he not go and get Richard's rubber from the classroom? He was certain, thinking about it, John would not have taken the rubber home. He had dozens of rubbers. No. He would have put it in his tray so that he could take it out next day and bait Sam with it. He might even use it. Sam guessed, rightly, that John thought the rubber may have magic powers that would help him do work as good as Sam's.

The new Sam was not concerned with rules and he had no sooner thought about it than he had done it. He walked boldly through the doors and into school. As quick as a wind-blown leaf he was in the corridor and on the way to the classroom. Once there he paused. Slabs of moonlight lay like thin metallic carpet on the concrete, but in between was darkness that Sam felt was solid.

He stayed still for several seconds almost afraid to step into the thick broth of shadow. The moonlight seemed unable to dilute the dark or spread itself. While he was still he heard the eager home going tap-tap-tap-tap of the cleaner's shoes on the entrance hall tiles. Unable to do anything or move Sam heard the rapid urgent bleeps of the burglar alarm that guarded the offices and video room. Then a glow of electric light died far down the corridor and a key turned very decisively in a lock. He was locked in the school. Sam found he was licking his lips which tasted salty and bitter.

For some time Sam remained where he was, like a visitor surveys a planet that has never before been visited. He became acutely aware of all the clicks and draughts in the building. The place was alive when it was quiet, alive in a way that Sam had not dreamed was possible. A heating pipe clicked and then clanged in the hall. A rose bush scratched at the window, as if wanting to join the invisible party in the dark. The library clock could be heard noisily jerking its fingers, its quartz crystal vibrating time signals to unseen ears.

A secret life was emerging that the children during the day were unaware of. Perhaps the building soaked up the energy of the children who were there during the day. Sam had not expected to be surrounded with such hidden life. It was another surprise in his cold new world.

Eventually he moved forward on tiptoe as though in the presence of some mysterious and uncertain force. Escaping did not concern him. There was a window at floor level in the classroom that opened out to grass. One wet dinnertime when the dinner ladies were elsewhere John had made Lisa Elliot get out and stand in the rain for five minutes because she had got in his way when he was trying to be first at the wet dinnertime games cupboard.

The classroom did not breathe the half spoken vibrations that the rest of the school did. Looking round the familiar room Sam thought it looked more like a dark negative belonging to a colour print. The room was familiar but the colours were not. Sam shut the door to keep out the greater forces he had felt down the corridor. He discovered he was shaking a little. He stared at the moonlit room with its shades of brown and blue and the slanting squares of silver light that dimmed and brightened as clouds passed over the moon.

He was never quite sure of what happened next or why. He knew after the Big Bang the Universe had probably been shaken by nuclear explosions as new worlds and stars were born. Perhaps it was like that. Or perhaps it was the negative image of the classroom where everything had changed. And Sam was different in a different world in a room that looked different. Like the classroom he changed and flipped to the opposite of his original self. He strode over to John's tray and yanked it out with uncaring force, unheeding of the squeal of breaking plastic. The tray fell with a bang into the thick shadow along with John's possessions. But the rubber was there, a dim square pearl in the night and Sam picked it up and carefully stuffed it in the back pocket of his jeans.

Then came the nuclear brainstorm in the changed world of moonlight. Sam caught sight of the golden, swollen, mad bird on the front of John's cuckoo project. His lips curled in sheer contempt. John was useless, hopeless where drawing was concerned. He picked the folder up and sneered mentally at it. Then he ripped it in half. John had used so much of Sam's gold pen on the bird that it was like gold leaf. As Sam tore away in the moonlight a cloud of sparkling gold dust surrounded him like radioactive fallout. The folder lay in scattered fragments at his feet.

Breathing heavily Sam bent to pick up the leather boot pencil case that to the class was John's badge of power. He undid it, damaging the brass zip in his meltdown of anger. He took out a handful of felt and fibre tips, expensive roller balls, and threw them round the room. He did this several times and they rattled round like shrapnel after an explosion. An owl, pausing on a tree outside, wondered at the frantic cuckoo-chick heavings of the creature within the classroom, fighting, it seemed, for existence. The last felt tip flew through the air like a silver missile in a Star War and landed upright in the roses on Mrs Firth's desk.

Sam threw some more of John's belongings about and then the reaction was spent. His anger cooled as rapidly as a fireball in deep frozen space. He just wanted out now. Coldly, calmly, he walked over to the window, undid the latch and climbed over the low sill. Then he gently slammed it and heard the soft click as the window locked itself. His mind still uncaring he decided to break another rule. The Big Bang had transformed him completely. He would cross the school field and squeeze through the hedge into York Road. (Breakage of this rule usually reduced Mrs Stone, the deputy head, into twitching splutterings and eye-bulging lectures.)

Four minutes later Sam was opening the back door and finding Richard with his coat on and the annoyed Spot on his lead. Richard, knowing his mother was still close to flashpoint, gave Sam a wide Judas smile.

'I was just coming out to look for you.' Richard was aware of warning looks from both his mother and father. 'All right, Sam?'

'Yes thanks,' said Sam. 'And I'll take the dog.' He suddenly felt in control in this sad new world. 'I can see a few stars now.' He suddenly realized it was John's night for martial arts lessons. He had frequently boasted about it and how his dad took him for a meal afterwards. Sam turned to Richard. 'Here's your precious rubber that you can't seem to live without. It's a pity it's replaced that girlfriend you fell out with.'

Richard caught the rubber and was about to make a clever remark when the door shut in his face and he saw his mother's look.

'You see, I told you there was nothing really wrong,' said Sam's mother drowsily in front of the fire. She had her feet up and sounded more like her own self. 'He just needed a little time to himself. It's all sorted out now. I knew it would be.' She gave a contented look of triumph at her husband and turned back to the interesting problems of *Brookside* on a tape saved from the previous week.

TWELVE

The surprises of the moonlit world slowly faded into a sparkling sunlit autumn morning with spiders' webs shimmering with drops and competing with Mrs Snow's diamonds. In her kitchen the brilliant low sunlight lit up the antique copper pans that hung round the kitchen—polished to red-gold mirrors by the daily help. On the windowsill an elegant cut-glass decanter held the dregs of last night's claret, the cut glass making nests of rainbows on the marble work surface. It was a startling contrast to Sam's moonlit adventures of the night before.

Mrs Snow faced John across the sunlit table, a genuine smile of contented affection and love upon her face. Diamond studs flashed in her ears and her well cut suit was razor sharp against the sunlight. She took her eyes away from her chick and with a sharp click opened her personal organizer. Keys rattled softly like a world war of snails as she keyed in her passwords. She was blissfully unaware of the terror John was feeling, a dread of the test results. She gave John a tender smile.

'I'm just confirming the time of my twice termly appointment with your Mrs Firth. (She made Mrs Firth sound like a parcel of lost property.) As you know, chicken, I like to check your progress with your teacher before the actual open evening. Open evening does not come soon enough for me, as I have often told Nancy Highfield. (The headteacher was neatly labelled, rather like a silly young girl of twelve.) I like to know what is going on. I want to see your work now.'

John was bathed in a loving smile. It was, after all, her way of seeing John had the very best out of his education. But the smile made John flinch as if she had smacked his face instead. His eyes avoided the bright warm beams of her smile.

'There's only a cuckoo project worth looking at,' John mumbled. 'We've not done much really.' He stared miserably out of the window where a jackdaw was carrying away the remains of his parents' supper from the bird tables.

Mrs Snow rose from her chair smiling. She gave her Italian silk scarf a light adjustment. Sunshine dazzled John's eyes as it was captured then reflected from the jewelled snake on her lapel. Everything, she felt, was as it should be this beautiful morning.

'Are you ready for school, John?'

John was seized by a desperate late panic attack. He produced a hastily strung collection of wildly feeble excuses. He dreaded his mother going to school. He was ashamed of his work and the thought of his mother's long cool fingers sifting his work chilled him with horror.

'I haven't got my school bag. I've lost it.'

Mrs Snow followed him out of the kitchen, her smile waning a little. Like a cross hedgehog, the prickles of irritation that her schedule might be spoiled soon poked through the feelings of love. However, she had a lawyer's instinct and a mother's intuition that John was not telling the truth. She sailed straight into John's bedroom and sank gracefully to her knees and felt under the bed. She produced John's bag and gave it to him as though it were a final proof in a murder trial.

'I forgot. I need clean shorts. I'm not going without them. Mrs Firth will yell at me all morning.'

The loving smile remained but tightened a fraction. She crossed the landing to the linen room and produced a whiter than white pair from a neat pile. She handed John the shorts without a word. John knew this was a signal of great danger, but he was past caring. He knew a visit to school would devastate the next few weeks. The words 'good private boarding school' would buzz in the air again. John swallowed hard. His breakfast was unwilling to settle this morning.

'I need a pen.'

Sighing, but still smiling—just—Mrs Snow opened her handbag and gave John a plastic office pen. She always carried two cheap pens ready for the forgetful, the careless, and those on legal aid.

'I'll go and get the car out and then you will be quite ready.' This was a command not a loving enquiry.

John heard nothing for a time because her shoes were on the thick carpet of the stairs. Then he heard the warlike machine-gun stutter of her staccato heels on the handpainted ceramic tiles of the hall. After a while they returned. John staggered down the stairs. His legs felt like cotton wool. He collapsed on the hall settee, the one by the open fireplace that blazed with burning logs on the Snows' annual Christmas party. Mrs Snow was very proud of the hall. When she saw John collapsing on the settee and building a protective nest of cushions her smile was finally killed. He stared up at her with pleading eyes.

'I feel really bad, Mum.'

Mrs Snow looked at him in the manner she looked at evidence given by a young, inexperienced, nervous policeman in court. Of course, she had no worries. Illness was planned for. She had an hour before her first client, time to ring the doctor, time to arrange with Mrs

Crabtree, one of the daily helps, who could nurse John. She gave John a hug. She felt a surge of love for him. But neither the hug or the love prejudiced how she saw the case of John's illness. She knew he was not ill. Her cool cheek on his forehead had told her that.

'Now come along, darling. Sit up and take deep, deep breaths while I just fetch a case from the study.'

She returned carrying a soft black leather portfolio. John sat up, swaying a little. He attempted one last stand.

'I just don't feel up to school today. If you loved me you wouldn't send me.'

'Sweetheart, now come along do. You look fine to me. Is there something you'd like to tell me about school? Is there something bothering you? Are you worried over some test or other?'

John brushed the cushions aside and was on his feet at once.

'As for loving you, darling, well, the evidence is all around you. There's the new sports bag that Daddy bought you last week. You're wearing the new trainers you so badly wanted and I bought you two weekends ago. I've just prepared you a nourishing healthy breakfast. You were safe, secure, warm in your bedroom all last night and we were here if you needed us. Why, only last week in court I heard of a little boy who was left—'

John strode across the hall whispering foul language under his breath. Apart from Sam Wilkinson there was nothing John hated more than his mother's tales about abused or deprived children. Other children bored him rigid and the deprived made him feel angry and guilty in a way he could not fully understand. There was nothing else said until the big car arrived softly and confidently outside school.

'I'll go to the classroom now, darling, and check my appointment with Mrs Firth.'

An urgent phone call on the car phone from the Law Society in London saved John for the time being. Mrs Snow decided to contact Mrs Firth later that morning. John left the car angrily, his hand clasped so hard round the key to the flats that it brought blood. But John's need to lash out, escape, hurt and bully others made him quite unaware of the blood trickling down his fingers.

Mrs Firth arrived late for school, only the third time in thirty years. She ran into school clutching a Tesco bag crammed with tests and a Waterstone's carrier containing planning and curriculum notes. She had worked until eleven o'clock last night. She was tired, her anorak flapped in rhythm to her swinging carriers, and her hair stuck up where the brush and drier had missed. She pretended not to see the group of parents in the entrance. If she did not see them perhaps they would not notice her late arrival. She had been glad to see that Mrs Highfield was busy, bending over the water meter in the middle of the yard.

Some children were already heading up the corridor to the classroom. Mrs Firth was anxious to reach the classroom first and gritted her teeth as she prepared for overtaking strategies. She neatly hustled two children aside by using her carrier bags, giving them a sweet smile as she stepped in front of them. Now she was able to catch up Mrs Stone who was making a more organized walk to her room carrying a beaker of coffee. She stared at Mrs Firth as she bustled up and Mrs Firth, feeling sensitive, took this as criticism of her lateness. In fact Mrs Stone wanted to tell Mrs Firth her hair was sticking up but didn't dare. Mrs Firth began a long and windy account of her late arrival.

'The traffic, Jane! I thought I'd drive down Well Lane as I'd plenty of time and it's a pretty way but they're building new drains.' She walked with Mrs Stone in a way that effectively blocked the corridor. She sucked in more air. 'Then there had been an accident in Dale Drive and there was a *huge* tailback. It's *so* difficult to know the best way to get here early . . .' She saw there was a good chance of reaching the classroom first. There were only two of her children ahead of her. The rest were Mrs Stone's.

'Then, to cap everything, Jane, a bus had broken down on Vernon Hill just where the road is so narrow.' She raised her voice and shouted breathlessly, 'Alison! And you, Emma! Don't block the corridor while you stand and natter. Let Mrs Stone and me pass you, please. We've so much to do.' Breathless but triumphant she had reached the classroom door.

'I'll go and get you a coffee,' said Mrs Stone. 'There are plenty of parents doing activities in my room this morning. I won't be missed for a bit.'

'Oh, would you, Jane? That's so kind, dear. I was up till all hours with school work and I feel shattered before I even start.' She smiled at the children lining up behind her and opened the classroom door.

'Come along in, now. Hurry up. Some of you do dawdle. Books out.'

At first she did not notice there was anything amiss in the room. She went to her desk with the tunnel vision of someone who has too much to do. Then she saw the felt-tip pen poking out of the red roses as though ready for launching. For a moment she stared at it in disbelief thinking perhaps it was a symptom of her late night. But this momentary state of wakeful dreaminess did not last. Several children had followed her into the classroom. At first they were astonished into silence by the mess Sam had left. But their powers of recovery were quicker than their teacher's. They turned to exclaim to themselves and to Mrs Firth.

Mrs Firth unglued her gaze from the pen stuck in the heart of the roses and looked at what was causing the children to cry out. She stared in disbelief at the pencil case boot on top of the blackboard. Her mouth opened to a small and wondering O as she saw the golden eggshell remains of John's project on the floor. She gaped at the selection of pens balancing on the tops of the fluorescent light fittings. Her eyes wandered to see more pens on models and books all around the room. But then her gaze settled back on the pen that was stabbing the roses. It seemed to have a hypnotic effect upon her. As she stared, Sam walked into the room.

He showed genuine surprise. He had vaguely thought the cleaners or the caretaker would sort out the mess. The new Sam did not seem as intelligent as the pre-Big Bang Sam. Sam felt oddly detached, unconcerned, like a visiting observer to a new and chaotic universe. His old world had vanished for ever, it seemed. The cosmos had reformed. The new Sam felt uncaring, unloving, and unfeeling. He stared at Mrs Firth and the other children, his face a mask of indifference. Perhaps there were some fragments of the old Sam still intact, because something made him blush very, very slightly. But it was enough for some keen-eyed children to spot.

A deep sigh blew about the classroom like the first breath of wind over the sea before an ocean storm. There was a murmur of soft voices like choppy waves and then louder voices. This quickly swelled in volume to shouting, extremely loud shouts. Accusations, blame, wonder, advice, some rather nervous laughter filled the room with a hurricane of loud babble. Every child in the room realized that this was the start of a new chapter in school life. Nothing would ever be the same again. John Snow affected everybody's lives—he was like that. Six years' experience with him had taught everybody to expect the worst. Nervous excitement topped with worry made them turn to Mrs Firth with a hail of suggestions.

'Mrs Firth, shall Donna and me fetch the caretaker?'

'Mrs Firth, shall Jack, Robert, and me run for Mrs Highfield?'

'Miss, can I go round all the teachers and say you want a dustpan and brush?'

'Adam says he knows who's done this, Miss.'

'I don't like John but this isn't fair, Mrs Firth,' said Jenny, daring to say something she had wanted to say for years but adding a safeguard in case of later reprisals from John.

'Miss, Miss, Miss, can Darren, James, Andrew, and me go and get a ladder and climb on the blackboards and get those pens? We won't be long. Darren says his dad's got a ladder in the garage and he only lives—'

Mrs Firth clapped her hands loudly. 'Yes. I mean, no you may *not* fetch ladders. *Everyone sit down at once and leave everything where it is.* I said *sit down.* Jack, sit down, do you hear? Why you are racing round and round like a circus clown in a sawdust ring I do not know. You will spend the rest of the day holding my hand like a silly infant if you do not—'

She was aware that the silence she had requested had descended but it was not of her making. The class were looking towards the door. John was there. Hearing the joyous noise of chaos in the classroom had made him walk twice his usual morning speed. He was still shaking from his mother's planned visit to Mrs Firth and the uproar had hurried him along quickly. Perhaps a fire or a bomb had destroyed the classroom and the tests. He looked hopefully in the direction of the trays hoping to see blasted and charred remains of his work. Instead he saw his own tray, and his alone, thrown to the ground, its right-hand rim splintered and smashed.

Now the class became deathly still as they watched John's eyes move from looking at the thrown-down tray to the scattered shell of the golden cover and then towards his boot case on the top of the blackboard. They watched as John's usually well-fed indifferent expression changed to a look of wounded fury. It was the first time in six years at school that anyone had dared to touch his possessions. Rage mixed with the earlier despair and short-circuited in John's brain to full tantrum mode.

'You did this.' John turned on Sam who was still slightly pink like a felt-tip pen that balanced on the dictionaries behind him. No one else spoke. The pink colour left Sam's face. Fear entered his mind.

'*You did this. Pig!*' Sam stepped neatly sideways and put a table between himself and John. He knew, with cool and horrible intensity, that he was alone in the universe with John. 'You did this. And you'll pay for it. I'll see you pay for it.' John behaved exactly as his father had when a new car was scraped in the gymnasium car park. Blind anger made John repeat himself like an avenging cuckoo. 'You did it. You did it. You'll pay. You'll pay. And you know how you'll pay. And you know how you'll pay.'

Mrs Firth watched John helplessly. She did not see Sam turn from pink to corpse white. John had reacted so violently and with such speed that she had no time to defuse the situation.

'And as for you, you'd better listen, right?' John was speaking directly to Mrs Firth. His rudeness and speed of reaction dumbfounded Mrs Firth further. She had boasted that she could control John, never suspecting a situation like this could arise. 'I'm not putting up with this, do you hear me? Have you got that?'

Mrs Firth swallowed hard. Her earlier torpor vanished. She made a step forward and was hardly able to resist giving John a hard smack across his face. She made another step towards him but was mercifully saved from something terrible by John's next move.

'Right. Well, I'm clearing off. I'm not staying here to be insulted by the likes of him.' He gave Sam a dangerous look. 'I'll be back when he's (he stabbed a finger in the white-faced Sam's direction) cleared up what he's done and he's made me and written me and drawn me a new project for open evening. And he'd better get that ready for me quick. And you wait, Wilkinson. I'll make you wish you'd never been born. You ain't seen nuttin' yet.'

Nobody dared to laugh at the last bit of video speak. John walked towards the door. Sam dodged round the table again. John framed himself in the doorway and grabbed the door. He slammed it with the detonation of a bomb. The whole room experienced the blast. The pen in the roses sank to a horizontal position and the boot fell with a soft thud from the blackboard.

For several seconds there was a bomb-rinsed silence and then the sounds of the outside world filtered back into the crater of silence he had created. A police siren could be heard, then a bus revving up, two robins singing somewhere and challenging each other's autumn territory. A ray of sunlight caught the curled fragments of John's folder as they lay on the carpet.

Sam wondered at his lack of feeling. He felt cold, bleak, and disinterested. Somewhere a voice, echoing through endless space, past black holes and empty voids, warned him that John now posed a huge threat to him, but he felt numb with all his troubles, like fingers exposed too long to cold winds and frost. He turned to look at Mrs Firth, a mute appeal for help.

Mrs Firth was quickly preparing to reinvent her credibility. She wanted to forget and she wanted the class to forget how John had just insulted her. She could not cope with the threats to herself and Sam so she pretended they had not happened. Sam bore the brunt of her attempt to recover the situation.

'Help me to collect John's things, please. Or what's left of them. You are going to have to have a very long talk with Mrs Highfield about all of this. Now, help me pick up everything, please. And the rest of you can collect your books and read in *silence*. Have you heard me, Jack? Do I have to hold hands with you as you read?'

Silence and a battered sense of order fell into place in the room. Sam picked everything up in the classroom with sidelong glances at the other children who were obediently still and silent but were certainly not reading. Sam's status had subtly changed and the class watched eagerly for the next moves. The battle between John and Sam had now become theatre, as good as a video or a favourite soap. Sam finished picking up the fragments and then stood quietly by Mrs Firth as she scribbled a rapid note for Sam to take to the headteacher.

When Sam had left with the note there was a ripple of excitement round the room in the same way that small birds mutter or twitter when cuckoos or hawks pass high in the skies.

'Go back to your reading at once,' commanded Mrs Firth. She had regained control. 'What goes on between Sam and John is none of your business.' But the class did not believe her.

THIRTEEN

Mrs Highfield reluctantly absorbed the fact from Mrs Firth's note that John had run out of school. Mrs Firth explained in some detail that Sam had torn up John's work and tipped the contents of his tray on the floor 'and thrown John's possessions in the air'. Mrs Highfield pretended to read the note slowly as she worked out a way of dealing with this unwelcome turn of events. She was acutely aware of the accusing eyes of Sam Wilkinson upon her as she read the note.

But her mind was really upon John and his mother. She knew that this would certainly result in the old threat from Mrs Snow that it was time John left the school. Nuisance as John was Mrs Highfield would rather he stayed. To have such rich and influential parents as John's was good for the school. They were generous with money. John's father sent his firm's accountants to help with the school budget—free of charge. Mrs Snow was a school governor and her letters often managed to get blood from stones. And the loss of a child, whoever he or she was, meant loss of money to the school budget. Mrs Highfield sighed vigorously and the draught stirred the hairs on Sam's head.

Still Mrs Highfield continued to pretend to read. She fought a desire to run after John. Usually she did not pursue runaways after the age of seven. Escaping children over that age ran too quickly. She refused to run and lose a race with long-legged juniors and stand red and breathless by the shops while they vanished down the road in a cloud of dust. As Mrs Snow would say, it was bad marketing for the school. No. She would not run after John. She was all in red today. Red dress, red earrings, red beads, and red shoes. The last time she had worn this outfit an infant had painted a red blob and written *Mrs Highfield* beneath it. Mrs Highfield had laughed merrily. Nevertheless she had stored it away in her memory. (The same child had drawn a brown twig and called it *Mrs Firth*. Mrs Firth had not laughed merrily.)

Mrs Highfield looked up at last, her face arranged into its *'we are very cross indeed'* expression. She took in a deep breath so when she spoke her voice would sound as stern as she felt.

'Did you empty John's tray, destroy his work, and throw his things about?'

Sam did not reply. She could not help him and he knew she had made up her mind anyway. A tense silence invaded the room.

'Well, you're not denying it so I can only assume that you did. What you did was quite unacceptable. It was very wrong. When John is found you will be punished.'

It was clear the biggest problem was John. Sam came second, he could see that. Sam remained silent. He saw little purpose in communicating with people in this drab new world. He stared at Mrs Highfield, his eyes dull and his mouth firmly closed. Mrs Highfield removed her reading glasses in the hope that her naked glare would stir Sam to say something. The glasses swung gently but crossly on a gold chain round her neck. In fact she was beginning to focus on Sam. Children who refused to talk always brought out the worst in her. Usually sensitive to the needs of children, she failed to sense the despair beneath Sam's sullen looks.

'I do not want you to return to the class until I can

126

see some signs that you are sorry for what you have done to John's work. I am going to have to do a great deal of explaining to John's mother.' This was almost a cry for help from Mrs Highfield but Sam was unmoved. 'You had better sit outside at a table in the library and read a book. I hope for your sake that John returns before ten o'clock because if he does not I shall have to ring the police.'

Sam seemed a lot less worried about Mrs Snow and the police than Mrs Highfield. Sam left the room closing the door softly behind him. Mrs Highfield fidgeted. She twiddled the chain of her glasses and wound a strand of her hair round her finger. She tried to look at some new tests, the teachers' salary bill for the month, the electricity bill, some new reading books. But always Mrs Snow's face appeared on the papers or pages. She nearly prayed for John to return. If only he would come back, knock on the door, say he was sorry, as he usually did, then she could send him to his class and deal with Sam. Mrs Snow would never know. But the clock jerked quickly to the hour of ten and John did not appear.

Mrs Highfield gave a sigh that was close to a sob and asked the school secretary to find her Mrs Snow's office telephone number. Then she keyed in the number as slowly as she could hoping and hoping that John would knock and apologize with his usual smooth charm. But now the friendly sing-song of the receptionist at the barrister's office dashed her hopes further. Things were sliding downhill to trouble very quickly. Everything was out of control.

'Good morning, Brown, Pipit, and Snow, Barristers. Tracey speaking. How can I help?'

'I need to speak to Mrs Snow. It concerns a serious personal family problem for her.'

'Mrs Snow is with a client at the moment. If you could give me your number I will see she contacts you the moment she is free.'

'I am afraid that will not do. This is a *most* urgent matter. My name is Nancy Highfield. I am the head-teacher of Crossroads Primary School where her son is a student. I need to contact her at once concerning her son. It cannot wait.'

Mrs Highfield could hear Tracey suck in air like a diver before plunging into dangerous waters. Tracey knew the terrible consequences of interrupting Mrs Snow when she was with a client. People had been sacked for less. But Tracey was brave, she bit her lip and put Mrs Highfield through to Mrs Snow who answered in a voice as dangerous as splinters of cut glass.

By half-past ten Mrs Highfield was visibly shaking in her red shoes. In the library Sam looked at astronomy books but found facts did not give him the pleasure they once did. The phone call had been worse than anything Mrs Highfield had imagined. The police had been called. Mrs Snow had used this as one of her many dagger thrusts of anger over the phone.

'You do know, Nancy, that any parent seeing the police in school may well think of removing their child. And every child is worth at least a thousand a year to you.'

Mrs Highfield stood distractedly by her door and did not even hear Sam ask if he could go to the lavatory.

Mrs Highfield watched the sleek gleaming car enter the parents' car park and felt close to tears. She suddenly thought that it was not Sam who was being bullied it was *her*. Anger and self pity overwhelmed her. What had happened? She had loved being with children, teaching them to read, showing them books, finding out exciting things, talking to them, sharing their hopes and problems and now she was being *bullied*. All she wanted was to be with children and enjoy herself. She saw the expression on Mrs Snow's face as she locked the car and Mrs Highfield covered her face with her hands.

Sam saw Mrs Snow enter the building like the meteorite that destroyed the dinosaurs, landing in Mrs Highfield's room with a door slam that her son could not have bettered. Next came a policeman, his radio crackling but whether with static from Sam's own Big Bang or Mrs Snow's entrance, Sam was uncertain. Loud and angry voices reached Sam's ears through the door like rumbles from distant stars. Eventually Mrs Highfield almost ran from her room, still talking.

'We'll go to John's classroom now. Sam, come to the room with us. He may be able to help,' she said over her shoulder to Mrs Snow and the policeman.

Mrs Highfield had not blamed Sam—yet. She would protect Sam as long as she could. The main thing was to find John. Mrs Snow looked at Sam with the expression she reserved for stray baked beans (fortified with vitamins) that sometimes fell from John's plate when he ate close by his mother. Mrs Highfield led the way in her red dress followed by Mrs Snow breathing out fury and Chanel perfume, then Sam, then the policeman crackling at the rear.

They lined up before the class like visiting royalty. The class were spellbound by this real-life drama before them that excelled anything *Neighbours* could offer. Mrs Highfield spoke with care. Despite her conviction she was being bullied she still tried to care for the children and Sam was spared a little longer.

'John has run away from school this morning. We think he may have done this because somebody interfered with his private possessions. We are very worried about his safety. If any of you can say anything that might help us to find John we would like to hear from you.' She smiled a faint weary smile like reluctant winter sunshine.

'Mrs Highfield, I know who did it. It was—'

'No, Lora. We want to find John. I shall ask who did it later. Now please be quiet, Lora.'

Lora fell quiet under the majesty of Mrs Highfield. The class was silent too. Talking about John was a minefield few were prepared to walk on. There was a long and uncomfortable silence. The policeman blew out his cheeks and time passed. Mrs Snow watched the class with an expert eye searching for blame. She was well aware that most of the class were looking at Sam with a mixture of interest, awe, and wonder. Seeing this Mrs Snow turned on him.

'Aren't you the boy who defaced the property notice?'

Sam stared at her. He'd forgotten about that. A year ago Mr Snow had bought a house next to the church. A notice had gone up saying TO LET. Sam and Adam used a thick felt-tip and made the board say TOILET by inserting a letter I. They had the satisfaction of seeing a gang of old ladies heading for the house after a coach had brought pensioners to the church for a fellowship meeting. Mrs Snow had found out and Sam and Adam had had to wash away the I during one playtime. Adam, fearing Mrs Snow would remember him, tried to be helpful.

'I think I know where John could have gone.'

'Right,' said the policeman sounding relieved. 'Are you his best friend?' Adam gave Sam a quick look and nodded. Sam felt nothing at all. 'Well,' said the policeman, 'you come along with us for a minute or two. Anyone else can help?' Again there was a silence. Nobody else dared to get mixed up with the tangle of barbed wire that was Mrs Snow and John. The policeman saw there was no point in staying where they were and the procession returned to Mrs Highfield's room.

Once inside Mrs Snow, desperately worried by John's absence, turned on Sam.

'Are you in John's class?'

Sam nodded at her.

'Why were you not at the party?'

Sam shrugged his shoulders, curled his lips. Mrs Snow simmered with worry and rage.

'I asked you a question. I want an answer, not a shrug.'

There was a very long silence. Mrs Snow tossed her brazen curls. There were tears in her eyes. 'What a rude little boy. I do not think much of the way you teach manners and spoken English, Nancy. If you will not speak, Sam, or whatever your name is, I must draw my own conclusions. John did not want you at his party. I knew there was one boy short but John insisted there was not. It is easy for me to see that you are the boy who has made John run away—'

The policeman cleared his throat. This would not find John. But Mrs Snow was an expert at brushing unwanted policemen aside.

'It looks to me as if you have been persecuting John. He has run away to hide from you. You will be in very serious trouble for being the reason for his leaving.'

Sam could say nothing. He wondered a little at the brightness of her tears and the diamond earrings. The policeman and Mrs Highfield looked on helplessly at Mrs Snow's tearful anxious reaction. Mrs Snow, blinking her eyes, turned to Adam. Honey and sunshine mixed with the tears.

'Hello, Adam dear.' Mrs Snow knew she was an expert at dealing with child witnesses in court. 'Do you know where John might have gone?'

'He has a den.'

'A den,' sighed Mrs Snow with mock enthusiasm in a patronizing See-how-well-I-talk-to-children-voice. 'Now, Adam. Could you possibly tell us where this den is?' She gave a tearful smile. She knew Adam was going to say up by the rhododendron bushes, close by the little wood of laburnums.

'He has a den in the flats. He says he's going to—'

'Oh no, no no no no, he has not. That may be his little fantasy but he has no den outside the garden. I'm a barrister you see (she gave the policeman a triumphant look) and I see what happens to children when they are unloved or neglected. John is *never* allowed out on his own. Except today.' She gave Mrs Highfield an accusing glare and then a tear escaped and ran down the smooth and perfect cheek.

Adam blushed red and refused to speak again. Sam cleared his throat.

'He has got a den in the flats. He says he's going to make—'

'Oh really, Nancy, and you, constable, we are wasting valuable time. John has never been anywhere near those awful flats and certainly has not got a den there. I think these boys should return to class and work. The important thing is to find John. (She had to find a handkerchief.) I will ask John why he ran away when he is found.' She gave Sam a viperish stare.

'Thank you, lads,' said the policeman.

Mrs Highfield, feeling more bullied than ever by Mrs Snow, tried to gain control of the crisis.

'Go back to your classroom, boys.'

'I'll go and start things moving,' Sam and Adam heard the policeman say as they walked slowly away. 'We've given him another hour to return and he hasn't. Firstly we'll check those flats. (They heard a damp snort from Mrs Snow.) We would have done that anyway as a matter of course . . .' They heard the policeman's defiant tones fade as they walked through the library. They walked back to the classroom careful to walk a metre apart and say nothing to each other.

The children in the class hummed and buzzed like bees in a hive that has been rattled. Excitement and chaos electrified the atmosphere. Some, like Sam, felt they were in a new universe. Sam went to his place and saw the class were doing maths and he dutifully got out his maths book. He slowly became very aware of a subtle change in the classroom. During the time he had been John's Number One Victim the class pretended he did not exist. They knew that to talk to Sam would provoke an attack by John of one kind or another. But today things had changed. Sam had thrown John's things about and struggled against him. Today they saw Sam as a friendly alien but still not one of them. They were still uncertain how things would turn out. From bitter experience they knew John would bounce and bully back . . . but perhaps events were changing . . .

Nobody spoke to Sam during the dinner hour but when a football bounced against his trainers and he kicked it back and joined in nobody said a word. In the old world Adam and he had played their own games but the old times had gone. Sam played ferociously and felt better. Still nobody spoke to him directly but it was silence with a difference. Something had changed.

FOURTEEN

John ran out of the school gates as he had so often done before. But this time it was different. He did not head towards the summer house at the far end of his own garden. He had always taken refuge there before, away from the eyes of neighbours and cleaning ladies. The summer house was well sheltered by expensive shrubs, a cosy suntrap for Mrs Snow's summer 'barbies'. After an hour there he used to return to school, apologize with charm and fluency to Nanny Highfield and return to his class. But not today. This time John swerved into a narrow track between the houses and headed for the flats and the common. Today he had plans to carry out.

He ran all the way. Despite being a little overweight his visits to gyms and swimming pools made him reasonably fit. And his energy was fuelled by a powerful hatred for Sam Wilkinson. Violent, ugly, and unreal images flashed into his mind as he ran, things he would do to Wilkinson, a nasty patchwork quilt made from cuttings from his video collection. He was not going to let Sam get away with this. He would get Wilkinson into his den and sort him out. He was not going to be pushed around by the likes of Wilkinson. No way.

His breath came in angry spurts as he ran towards the flats. He thought about his project, the very best he had ever done and Wilkinson had wrecked it. Who did he think he was? He ground his teeth as he thought of his mother being told that another boy had touched and ruined his work.

He reached the flats and stopped and took in deep

breaths. Then he relaxed a little and lifted his face up to the September sunlight. John was not used to the simple pleasure of running and resting in the fresh air. He suddenly felt surprisingly happy with himself and was reminded of the never-to-be-forgotten evening in Spain when he had escaped. He stared up at the blue sky. He was not returning to school. He was going to sort things out for good. He would show everyone he was to be reckoned with, he would show Wilkinson in particular. Nobody was going to boss him about.

'No, sir!' he shouted loudly as he stood in the weed-filled car park. He took the key to the flat from his pocket and tossed it in the air where it glittered and revolved like a fantastic bird in flight. 'No, sir!' he shouted even more loudly, happily unaware he was copying his father overtaking a smaller car on the motorway or the New York cop in his favourite video.

He made his way confidently to the entrance of the flats where the door had been kicked in. Sunshine warmed and illuminated the entrance hall. Further in the air was colder and the smell of decay and worse things hung in the air. John was suddenly subdued. He halted at the foot of the stairs. He glanced down at the fake gold Rolex watch his father had brought him as a joke from Hong Kong. (John was proud of the watch and had fooled the whole class with its apparent authenticity.) The watch kept good time and said half-past nine.

John smiled in the half light. He knew Nanny Highfield would do nothing until ten. He smirked as he thought of the number of times he had returned and apologized. She always said she would not tell his mother if he had a good day in class. It had become a way of life. An enjoyable tantrum, spitting insults at other children, a free half hour before smooth glib apologies. But not today.

He felt pleased with himself again as he climbed the dusty gold stairs and let himself into the flat. The sun was shining right into what had been the lounge. A window was open and the air was fresh. John put his bag on a wobbly table. The bag had been gripped in his hand when he had yelled at Mrs Firth and he had not let go of it since then. He felt about under the card base of the bag and found what he wanted. It was an old wallet his father had thrown out when his mother had given him a brand new one off the huge tree in the hall at Christmas. John had rescued the wallet from the waste-paper bin in the study. He liked the smell of the expensive leather, the gold letters that said *Harrods*.

Inside the wallet was over £100. John's father was careless with money. It was a statement to the world that he was rich. Mr Snow watched over his credit cards but ten and twenty pound notes were stuffed everywhere. They were pulled out in pubs and for taxi drivers. They were left in the bathrooms by laundry baskets after a change of clothes. They were stuffed into a bedside drawer. John had taken one or two a week after he had found the key. The notes had not been missed.

John smiled. His plans were taking shape. He knew what he had to do and that was go shopping. He needed food. He needed light. He needed a weapon to protect himself and to control others. He saw that the Rolex said quarter to ten. There was no time to be lost. He needed to visit good shops, not like the ones in his own town. He would go to the nearby city where nobody would recognize him and buy food and weapons. Then he would creep back here and—'Yes, sir!'

Carrying the bag but with the wallet in his pocket he locked the flat and felt incredibly grown up. He ran softly and agilely down the stairs and once more faced the sun and the world at the flats' entrance. Again the sun warmed his face and the soft plumes of drifting thistledown and drowsy wasps added to his sense of well being. Then he set out.

'For Christ's sake!' said the bus driver to John when John asked for a ticket and gave him a twenty pound note for a fifty pence fare. The bus driver looked suspiciously at John wondering if the boy had been stealing, but looking at the expensive clothes decided John was some mad rich kid. John did not know how to react. It was the first time he had been on a public transport bus and the first time he had asked for a ticket for himself. He had been certain the bus driver would have been impressed with the twenty pound note offered.

John divided grown-ups into two classes, winners and losers, an idea he had absorbed from his father. Winners were doctors, lawyers, businessmen, and anyone with a car, jeep, or Land Rover 'worth over 20K'. Losers were shop assistants, street cleaners, gardeners, and teachers. And certainly bus drivers. John watched helplessly as the bus driver displayed his irritation and anger.

The driver handed him eighteen pound coins and handfuls of smaller coins. John filled his pockets and stood waiting for the ticket. 'There, mate!' shouted the driver pointing to a machine spitting out a ticket by the stairway to the top deck. John tugged at the ticket and was nearly sent spinning down the bus as the driver set off with a cross jerk. John was, however, untroubled. His great adventure had begun and he climbed to the top deck where he sat on a sun-warmed seat.

Bars of shadow passed across his now healthily flushed face as the bus made its way to the town centre. John enjoyed the view. It was surprisingly better than the car. He felt very pleased with himself. He had caught a bus well away from the flats and by houses he did not know. He had just walked till he came to a bus stop. Yes, sir! Things were going well. His Rolex told him Nanny Highfield would be dashing round now like a headless chicken and ringing for help. He smiled a self-satisfied smile.

He felt quite at home in the railway station. It had recently been renovated. Automatic doors, shining floors, matching seats, plants in earthenware containers, a fountain, display screens everywhere made John respect the place in a way he never respected school. He swaggered over to the ticket sales and demanded a first class ticket to the city. He had been on InterCity trains with his father and had watched him buying a ticket. John had not heard of family railcards or cheap returns. He thought first class was the only way to travel.

Like the bus driver, the ticket clerk studied John from behind his glass screen, a frown on his face. It was the first time a kid had asked for a first class ticket in all of his eight years working for the railways. He noted John's up-to-the-minute football shirt, designer tracksuit bottoms, expensive trainers and a flashy gold watch. He wondered to himself why some kids had everything and some were not even fed properly. He rudely asked John for the eighteen pounds without a please or thank you. When John handed over eighteen pounds, for a journey that only took half an hour on a fast train, the ticket clerk was convinced the kid was rolling in money from some rich family. He was totally convinced when he saw John's wallet with Harrods on it and a photograph of John himself on an identity window. He watched John stroll off to Platform Ten swinging a sports bag that he wouldn't have minded himself.

John caught an InterCity express and was given a free cup of coffee and called 'sir' by a stewardess who hardly noticed he was a young boy because she was thinking of nothing but her boyfriend. The woman guard on the train, clipping John's ticket, thought roughly the same thoughts as the ticket seller back on the station. 'Let me know if whoever's meeting you on the station doesn't turn up,' she said to John. John said nothing. He was unsure how to label her. She had a smart red suit and a hat, the kind his mother favoured for shopping. He could not decide if she was a winner or a loser. John left the station very content with the way things were going.

He made his way to an upmarket camping and outdoor pursuits shop where his father bought the equipment for their skiing holidays. John loved this shop. It was definitely for winners. He bought at once an army knife that had long been part of his fantasy life and daydreams. Next he bought a length of strong nylon rope and he smiled a horrible smile as he did so. He bought a sleeping bag that rolled up very small and was useful to pick up if you were running away in a hurry.

As soon as sixty pounds had been spent John felt a sense of deflation. It was always the same with shopping. It was fun going, it was great buying the stuff, but things never gave you the satisfaction you expected. John now wanted to return and get down to the real business of his fantasies. He bought another torch and then turned his mind to the buying of food.

He copied his mother and headed straight for Marks & Spencer's. He bought enough sandwiches to last two people for two days. He bought full fat sandwiches, prawns in mayonnaise, a seven hundred calorie ploughman's sandwich that his mother always forbade. As he added egg and cream cheese he almost heard her voice echo down the food hall. 'No, chicken. They're not good for you. It will give you heart trouble in your middle age as well as making you overweight now.' John smiled as he bought forbidden Danish pastries, a cream cake, and some full fat yoghurts. All the time he made sure he was buying enough for two. He gave his last twenty pound note to an uncaring cashier.

John found the carrier bag she gave him bothersome but he did not mind. He was in charge of his own life. He walked to the station blown along by the autumn wind and a daydream about the wild teenage boys asking him to join their gang at the flats and helping him to catch Wilkinson. He saw himself giving them money in exchange for keeping him hidden and saying nothing about his prisoner. Thoughts of being in control, giving out money and getting Sam, brought him to the station without realizing how tired and hungry he was.

He caught the right train but it was not an InterCity express. It took a long way round, stopped at every station, had no first class accommodation and was, John thought, more like a dirty old smelly bus than a train. The conductor did not even look at his ticket. For half of the journey the conductor had a ferocious argument with six students about off-peak fares and student railcards. Half-way through the journey the conductor changed places with another and he did not even bother to check the tickets of those already on the train. John was hot and thirsty and his body ached with the uncomfortable seat. His throat was dry and his eyes smarted.

He caught a bus back, careful to tender the exact fare, and was unnoticed. The bus was busy as it was rush hour. John was shoved up against a window, half hidden by his carriers and shopping, wedged in against a woman with a bag of what John thought must be ancient salmon. The journey seemed endless. John had to silence the voice within him that kept saying how nice a shower would be in his own private bathroom, how comfortable a settee in the lounge would be, how long and cool a drink from the fridge would be, how pleasant it would be in the big lounge with the curtains half drawn against the sun.

It was late afternoon when John approached the flats from the opposite side to his own house by houses he did not know. He entered cautiously through a little path through a wood behind some houses. He was glad he had been careful because he saw the police car before they saw him. He hid behind a tree but he was careless with tiredness and did not notice his carrier bags stuck out.

He remained there for some time, hot and bothered even though by now the sun had vanished into clouds. He watched the police car parked by the fire exit of the flats. The policemen were eating something and John's mouth watered. Suddenly the radio crackled, the policemen became alert. A voice, distorted and crackling, gave the men an important message about the missing boy—but John could not hear this. After this the car revved up, dust spurted from the back tyres, and it roared away. John stared after it thinking what a tinny cheapo car it was.

He waited five minutes then slowly made his way through the seeding thistles and parched nettles to the front entrance. He waited for several minutes in the pungent shadows of the entrance hall, making sure he was unobserved, then climbed the stairs to his den. He desperately wanted a drink of the raspberry and orange juice he had bought—but it was right on the bottom of the bag. It was cool inside his flat. He felt better. He had done it. He had reached his den without anyone seeing him.

But John was mistaken. Eyes watched him, eyes that were angry, amused, uncaring, and very intent. One pair of eyes, pale blue like the sky between clouds over the flats, belonged to the teenager who delivered the free paper to John's house, the boy so admired by John. The boy would deliver the paper this week with the headline LOCAL WEALTHY BUSINESSMAN PLEDGE—I'LL DEMOLISH THE FLATS AND THE YOBBOS WILL GO WITH THEM. Underneath would be a picture of John's smiling father.

Another pair of eyes the colour of the faded September leaves, another the colour of the grey clouds, yet another pair the colour of the sun on the tree trunks, all of them exchanged glances with the blue eyes of the paper boy. Nothing was said but everything was understood.

John had drunk a bottle of juice that was still pleasingly cold. Fresh air blew in at the window. John felt restored and he delved into his bag and brought out the army knife. It was at this precise moment there was a soft knock on the door of his flat. John held the knife poised in surprise. Then the soft, almost polite, knock came again.

'Whatever has happened we must do our work and not fall behind,' said Mrs Firth as afternoon school began. 'I'll do the register and then we'll make our way to the video room so we can press on with our project. And for heaven's sake, Jenny, give your mouth a rest. In the last five minutes you've said more than you have the whole time you've been in my class. I cannot think why you're so chirpy.'

Sam let out a little sigh of relief. He had half expected

to be told to make John a new folder. But Mrs Firth seemed to be more interested in the unusually noisy class on the way to the video room. 'I think someone's put something in their drinking water,' she said to Mrs Davidson whom they passed in the corridor. Sam flopped down in the middle of the floor and was not kicked or secretly shoved to the front row. He found himself almost enjoying the film. He could watch without neck ache and could not see the tiny lines that made the picture.

The pipits were now frantic trying to care for the bulky expanding chick. Everything the pipits brought was devoured, sometimes the cuckoo almost snapped the pipits' heads off as they rammed food down the big red throat. A chaffinch that had finished breeding her chicks and a blackbird that had also finished, began to bring food for the monster.

One bright morning the chick waddled away from the nest, took a few uncertain steps, flapped its wings and then flew uncaringly away. It did not return. It flew into some nearby trees and hissed and bubbled and was surprisingly brought food by a variety of birds. Three confident magpies brought it food and so did a jay. The film showed the unhappy pipits moping round their shattered nest with ruffled feathers and sad eyes. The parasite had left their lives for ever but they were grief stricken.

Sam spent a tranquil time drawing the cuckoo flying away, charting its route to the south coast and so to Spain where, Mrs Firth said, it would rest before it finally set out for Africa.

'Then it will return in spring and everything will begin all over again because that is nature's way,' said Mrs Firth cheerfully and contentedly.

The class were incredibly loud that afternoon. Mrs Firth wondered if they were worried and tense over the disappearance of John. It was the longest he had ever stayed away. With every passing minute both teacher and children saw John's disappearance becoming a serious crisis. Anything could happen to a runaway child.

Sam received a summons from Mrs Highfield to see her before he ran home. Two of the class said, 'See you, Sam,' as he left the classroom. He had not heard those commonplace words for days and days. As he left the room Sam thought the noise in the class was like a stormy sea. To Mrs Firth it was like a bursting dam. Torrents of words were spouting from children who had hardly spoken in class before.

Sam quickly found himself in another flood. This time it was the flood of unhappiness that spilled out of Mrs Highfield. All through the day she had kept receiving telephone calls from Mrs Snow. Mrs Snow was now frantic with worry and during each sobbing call she told Mrs Highfield exactly what she thought about the school, about Mrs Highfield as a headteacher, and what a failure the school had been for John. Tears of despair had trickled down Mrs Highfield's cheeks during the later conversations as Mrs Snow became more bitter and distressed.

During the last phone call Mrs Snow had jerkily explained that local television had announced John's disappearance at lunchtime. Some journalists must have heard and had telephoned Mrs Snow from the *Mirror* and the *Sun*. Mrs Snow had said she would explain everything to the papers—that was the least Mrs Highfield deserved. Mrs Highfield found herself shaking as she thought of possible headlines. SCHOOL BULLY BOY DRIVES KID TO LEAVE HOME. She raged at Sam.

'. . . I dare say you thought you were being bullied

when you came to see me. But they were trivial and unimportant things. You should have ignored them. What you did to John was much more serious. It is you, Sam Wilkinson, who is a nasty bully . . .'

She had to stop talking or else tears would have flooded out to join the word torrent. The mask of indifference slipped from Sam's face to reveal anger.

'I don't see how you can call me a bully. John Snow is bigger than me and the whole class knows he has got away with murder for years and years.'

'It seems to me, Sam, you did not learn anything from our bullying project last term. You are a great deal cleverer than John Snow. Your school work is generally the best in the class and you showed utter contempt of John's work by destroying it. *That* is *bullying*.' Her voice was close to a wail of misery and despair at the problem and the way it was growing. 'And the way you sneaked into school—some would say broke in—is *very* serious.'

Sam stared at her in disbelief. He felt like a visitor from Mars being taken round a human zoo and not understanding why the creatures on Earth behaved as they did. It was beyond belief. But Mrs Highfield was sailing off again on the floodtide of emotions.

'I shall consider excluding you from school. You broke in after school hours and destroyed property. I shall talk to the governors and the Chair and see what is to be done.'

Sam was now certain the woman and the world were mad. Now she was going to talk to the furniture about him. He left the room without a word and banged the door the way John would have done.

Sam arrived home with his throat feeling as if he had drunk burning oil. He had raced home because he was terrified John would be waiting to get him. Sam had no confidence the police would catch John before John caught him. Sam bounded upstairs and flopped on his bed and wondered if his heart was going to burst. Serve everyone right if it did, he thought. They'll all be sorry if they find me dead from a heart attack, he breathlessly whispered to the room.

By the noise below it sounded as if the whole family was at home. His father seemed to be at home all the time now. Sam did not understand why, he had been busy with his own problems. His mother was home earlier than usual and he could hear Richard and her arguing loudly. Then he picked out the voice of his oldest brother James. James had had a holiday job in another town and was now home ready to return to university. Sam made a rude gesture with his fingers when he heard his name called. He felt he could not be bothered with anybody any more. And it began as soon as he entered the room.

'Hello, love. I hear John Snow's run away,' was his mother's greeting to him. She was carving a joint of meat in honour of James who had been living, so he said, on baked beans and oranges for five weeks.

Sam nodded and slipped into his place. The post-Big Bang Sam said few words.

'Good riddance,' said Richard calmly. 'Can I have the crisp salty bits from the ends, Mum?'

'Richard!' said his mother genuinely shocked. 'To have a child go missing these days is an awful thing. God knows what might happen to them, you hear such dreadful things. When did this happen, Sam?'

Sam wrinkled his nose, stretched his fingers, shrugged his shoulders and looked at the ceiling. The meal proceeded with a great deal of talk about John but Sam did not join in. Once or twice he was aware of James's stare in his direction. He did not mind because James was the favourite brother. There was a gap of eight years between them and James had always been kind to him. The big age gap had prevented the tussles Sam had with Richard. Richard and Sam were like two competing fledglings in a nest. The noise in the room grew as the family ate and talked but Sam pretended to watch the television in the corner which was on, though he could not possibly hear it. But when the news came on John was the lead item. His mother turned up the sound.

'An eleven-year-old boy has gone missing today after running out of his school after an alleged misunderstanding with another pupil. The missing boy's parents have hinted at allegations of bullying within the school. The boy left Crossroads Primary School about nine o'clock and has been reported as buying a rail ticket to the city of—'

'God, I didn't think that mound of flab could run anywhere,' said Richard, his mouth full of third helpings.

'Listen, Richard,' said his mother. On the screen was a reporter with the policeman who had been in school earlier.

'We are now certain John is in the city somewhere. He was identified buying a ticket on the station video. The guard on the train travelling to the city has identified him from pictures shown to her. We have had reports of him purchasing goods in the city. We are certain he is somewhere in the city and the police there are on full alert. We are now seriously concerned for John's safety. In fact we are very worried. We are already combing derelict areas of the city, parks, and stations. Two boys went missing earlier this year and we think there may be connections with John's sudden disappearance.'

At this point Richard asked for fourth helpings, an advert came on, and the telephone rang. Sam's father turned the volume of the television down so the call could be answered. Sam got up and tried to leave the room but found his mother blocking the way by leaning up against the doorpost, rubbing her corn on to the other leg as she answered the phone. Sam could not escape. He sighed and folded his arms sulkily. He just wanted out of everything, the meal, the family, and now all this about John on the television. He listened to his mother.

'Yes, I recognized your voice, Mrs Snow. I'd like to say how worried and sorry we all are and if we can do anything—'

Everyone in the room was silent. They could hear the hard, dry, sawing caw of Mrs Snow cutting its way out of the telephone receiver.

'I'm sorry? I beg your pardon, Mrs Snow?'

The voice cut its way on. Mrs Wilkinson lowered the foot with the corn in delicate slow motion and listened on two feet. She blinked and they saw her turn and bite her lip.

'Sam did?'

The jagged babble that had started like a rook now rose in tone to a sobbing cuckoo-ish warble. Mrs Snow was now crying freely, telling the story as she knew it.

'Mrs Snow, I can't believe all this.'

The bubbling sobbing turned to an angry rasping filing note again. Mrs Wilkinson's expression turned from bewilderment to anger. She put the phone down with a jingling smack and turned to the listening family.

'Well, she's in a state. She's bound to be, poor woman, so would I be. But she's blaming you, Sam. She says you tore up his very best work and threw his things all round the school and you've been making his life a misery.'

Richard choked with delighted glee.

'And did you?' Mrs Wilkinson confronted Sam. There was a long silence. Sam did not know what to say. He looked at his mother and sensed she thought he had let the family down. The Snows and a few other families high on the hill were regarded as rich and successful. Sam felt his own misery was not being properly considered. 'And did you?' asked Mrs Wilkinson again.

Sam gave the tiniest of nods.

'Good for you, littl'un,' shouted Richard during a pause in eating and choking. 'It's about time someone stood up to that sack of—'.

'Don't even think of saying it, Richard,' said his mother. 'And for goodness' sake shut up, Richard. You're not too old to be given a good hiding.' Richard laughed happily and playfully put his fists up to his mother and boxed the air. His mother turned to Sam again. 'Well of all the things to do, Sam. I thought you'd got more between the ears, I really did. I thought you were the clever one in this family. And to spoil his things, John Snow of all people.'

'The boy has to learn to stand up for himself,' said his father quietly. 'Everyone knows that John Snow is a nasty bit of work. Sam needs to look after himself. Nobody else will.' His voice trailed away, lost in bitterness about his own life of no jobs and everything going wrong.

'Standing up for yourself does not mean ripping up someone else's book,' shouted Sam's mother. 'But that's you all over, Keith. Settle things with your fists first. Like that time in the pub. And look where it's got you. Nobody will give you a job—'

Sam dodged behind her and ran from the room. He knew the symptoms of a family row and this had the makings of a three star family row with his mum and dad centre ring. He could see himself being used by both his parents to score points against each other in the coming conflict. He hated that. He understood that this was going to be a row about the fact there were no jobs. His bullying of John Snow was a gloss on deep grievances. Sam ran down the hall. His foot was on the second step when he felt a heavy hand on his shoulder. It was James.

'Don't worry, Spud.' He used the name he called Sam when, as a baby, the family had first adopted him. Eight-year-old James had called Sam 'Spud' because he had a head like a big washed potato before it was baked in the oven. 'Don't worry, Spud. If that kid ran away because you tore up his project on goldfish, or whatever, he's just using it as an excuse to run away from something else. You don't run away for just that. He's running from something bigger than your carving up his art. It's not you that's to blame. Don't worry. See you later. I'm off to the pub for a game or something. I can do without all that grief in there.' He nodded towards the sound of shouted arguing from his parents.

Sam watched him go. It was the first kind word he had heard all day and for some strange reason it made him cry. He ran up to his room before Richard could spot him and closed the door and curled himself up on his bed. He had thought at eleven he had finished with crying but he was wrong. Then he fell asleep.

He awoke to hear the sound of Richard's radio through the wall of his room. The local news was on and he could hear every word. He heard that some shoppers in Marks and Spencer's in the city had seen John buying food and that extra police were now combing the city looking for him. The police had checked the station

150

videos on the InterCity platforms. John had not returned on an InterCity train. It was certain he was in grave danger.

A mad sense that he was to blame suddenly filled Sam's brain. They would blame him for all of this. He rolled over and covered up his ears.

FIFTEEN

For some time Sam remained on the bed, his eyes swollen, his head aching, and his nose tightly blocked. He watched the sky darken through a hundred shades of blue and knew that soon there would be stars. But he did not move. What was the point? At eight o'clock the door burst open and Spot entered carrying his lead. Spot was the happiest soul in the house at that moment because he had been given the remains of the dinner and gravy. Sam bent down to pat the dog and something in his mind sprang back to life. It was time to go out. John was safely out of the way. No. Safe was the wrong word but Sam could not help a faint smile. James was right. It was *not* his fault. John had started it, after all.

He fondled the dog and Spot's tail lashed the side of the bed. There had been moments in the last hour when Sam felt he was to blame for John hiding in a dangerous city centre. He had actually begun to feel guilty. Perhaps it had been the knowledge that the adults were blaming him. He was losing sight of the terror John's threats had caused and replacing it with guilt. Well, thank goodness for James. He slipped Spot's lead on.

He would go out. There was no point in staying in. Richard was now playing CDs as loud as he dared and a friend had come. They were making silly jokes and laughing and slapping the wall. Sam did not like Richard's taste in music.

And yet as he went downstairs the guilt flooded back. 'It's not my fault,' he said as he went down the stairs with Spot who wagged his tail so violently he missed his footing on the last step and fell and rolled. 'No, it's not,' said Sam again wondering at the way guilt had replaced fear.

Downstairs the gas fire blazed and the television flickered through air solid with tension. It was very clear his parents were not speaking to each other.

'I'm taking Spot out,' said Sam, his words falling dully into the room like stones on to a frozen lake.

'Be careful,' said his mother with forced cheerfulness. Sam knew this cheerful tone was for the benefit of his father to show that she was not in the least bit upset by all that had been said. He realized that his so-called bad behaviour had long been swallowed up by greater problems in their own life.

Nobody cares, thought Sam letting himself out. The cool night air unblocked his nose and blew away some of the strange guilt that lingered. He tried to concentrate on the pleasure of being out with John out of the way. But he had to fight the odd sense of unease and blame that the world was not all right. He looked up at the sky and the first stars and saw the splinter of mirror behind the trees that was Venus savagely reflecting the sun. Yet still the shadow remained in his mind like some Black Hole. He shifted his gaze to Saturn which he knew was in the constellation of Aries. Even with light pollution from the town he might be able just to see the rings with his binoculars. The night was chilled and frost was in the air. This pleased Sam for stars were bright in frost. He walked quickly, aware of stars and guilt in equal measures.

Spot led with his waving tail showing the way, the tail wagging over a belly tight with meat and gravy. By the last lamp-post Spot found some bubble gum that someone had spat out. Spot began to chew loudly and with sloppy satisfaction. As they approached the dark bulk of the flats Sam could hear the dog chewing noisily as he rustled in the undergrowth. Sam followed the path known only to Spot and himself and was soon in the middle of the old play area.

Sam tilted his head back. It was the time of night when stars were appearing one after the other like a crowd entering a football stadium. Sam scanned the zenith with his binoculars and then slowly lowered the binoculars down towards the solid darkness of the flats. Venus was sinking fast over the flats. He would watch it set in the west over the flats before he turned south to stare at Saturn. Always he was on the lookout for UFOs, a space craft, or a comet no one else had seen, to be called Comet Wilkinson.

The triangle of stars called Libra, the Scales, was frostily bright. Sam could not understand why it was called the Scales but he liked the triangle of stars. It was neat. His arms were aching a bit now and he had a wobble. He had noticed more strange aches and pains since John had picked on him. He decided to walk a little closer to the flats. That way Libra would rest on the roof of the flats and help him to keep the stars in view. Then he would look at Saturn. The darker it was for that the better.

At first he thought the dark blob on the roof was a tawny owl for there was a colony in the grounds. But it made a curious sound. Sam considered that the strange sound was his own imagination but then Spot heard it and came bounding out of the bushes. The dog looked up to the roof and at once began a curious warning yapping not a bit like his usual bark. Sam had not heard Spot warn like this before. He thought the dog was being silly and bent down and smacked his nose until he was

154

silent. Sam was more interested than alarmed. He raised his binoculars and began to readjust the focus to stare at the curious object. It was an action Sam did not complete.

'Sam . . . come here.' Then came the rattling bubbling noise that had disturbed Spot so much. The voice had been that of John Snow.

Thrills of pure horror rippled down Sam's body. All the taunts and threats of being locked up exploded back in Sam's mind like rockets in a night sky. He felt his legs weaken and just as in the worst kind of nightmare he discovered he could not run away. He tried to take a few steps backwards but soon fell with a dry rustling crash into the dried remains of summer's end. The binoculars followed him, bouncing with two heavy punches on his chest.

Somehow John had tricked the police and his mother and was waiting here for Sam. That ugly noise had been someone laughing. John was waiting for him. He had got him at last. He thought he saw the dim light of a torch or candle at a window and thought of the gang. Sam could hear his own breathing now, asthmatic and hoarse. Fear completely paralysed his body. Spot, hearing the voice of John, recognized it as the boy he had seen before. The dog accepted it was now a usual part of the environment and plunged back to explore the bushes.

Sam lay on a crackling cushion of dew-wet stalks and brambles, quite unaware that dry nettles and brambles were raking his scrabbling trembling fingers. He felt as cold and as immobile as a marble statue, petrified by the closeness of John Snow. What a fool he had been to listen to the television. Now only his eyes could move in his static body and he was certain he could see a candle gleam in a room. Who, or what, was waiting for him drained all the life out of his body.

If only he could run, dash for cover, race away from whoever was waiting to get him up there. He found his eye hypnotized by the faint light in the window and he heard himself muttering 'No' over and over again.

Any moment now the action would begin. John would stand laughing and triumphant against the stars and whoever he had in there would race out and capture him. Sam's mouth, eyes, and brain all raced their separate ways. If only he could organize himself to run. God, he must run. Run. He tried to crawl and once he heard Spot bound up to him and snuffle in his ear. The dog thought Sam was simply exploring the nettle beds. Time seemed to cease. John's head remained above the parapet of the roof in a grim, mocking, watchful video still.

He became aware of Spot by his side licking the salt tears off his cold cheeks. How much or how little time had passed Sam was totally uncertain. But the dog had stopped playing and exploring. His bubble gum was gone. He was whining. Sam was aware that his own crying was echoing strangely round the flats. It took in fact two minutes for Sam to realize that the sound he had thought was John laughing was John crying. This new understanding did not release Sam's legs from their paralysis. He was still terror stricken. This was a new trick of John Snow's. It was an act. The dry harsh ripple was not real. Sam began to crawl backwards and a bramble ripped his face. It was a trick to lure Sam into the flats, he knew it was. Spot could sense the evil and danger. Spot gently licked the blood away from Sam's face.

Sam now found his body was released from its rigidity

but he was shaking and he could not move because of that. The noise John was making was horrible. He began to wonder if it was all a dream. He managed to shuffle backwards on his back for some metres but sensed he was unable to stand. Fear possessed his body. But it had subtly changed. Now all he wanted to do was to get away from the ugly noise John was making. It was like a horror video. The noise was compelling like some strange magic call. Sam could almost feel his body attracted to the noise and then he knew they would get him. He attempted to crawl now and made some progress away from the ghastly noise. It was like a sound net being used to capture him.

Further away he began to wonder at the sound. He was now deep in the bushes, he could not see the entrance, and his mind was clearer. He knew John was a good actor. Watching him creep and say he was sorry to teachers proved that. And yet . . . Every year he wanted a part in the school play or musical. Every year he was turned down and there was a spate of petty bullying, tantrums, all boiling up from his frustrated anger. Perhaps it wasn't even John after all? Still unable to stand after these thoughts, Sam crawled a little further. He had managed to put a safer distance between himself and the terrors.

'Sam . . . please . . .' The voice was more distant. But the fear surged back over Sam like a returning tide. John usually said 'please' when he wanted his own way. He must get away from this place, he must get away . . . Sam expected a gang to appear again and found his lips were as dry as if he had been in the desert. He began his pathetic slithering along the ground again. Despite the fact Sam had crawled thirty metres into the undergrowth he could still hear the strange shuddering sound. And still he could not be sure whether it was helpless laughter or dry desperate sobbing.

'Sam . . . please come up to me.'

Sam's own laboured breathing began to drown the distant voice. Spot was whimpering oddly in a strange way different again to a few minutes ago. He bumped up against the thick trunks of an overgrown laurel bush. Although his grip was weak Sam managed to struggle to his feet for the first time it seemed in hours. He must make it to the street lamp before the gang rushed out. John had some mysterious plan, he knew he had. In slow motion, not unlike a diver in deep water, Sam struggled along with the sound of the hysterical laughing-crying lapping round his own coarse breathing. Then he tripped and fell. At once the strange noise John was making ceased.

From the ground Sam saw he was no longer visible from the roof. He gave a low moan. John was coming down after him. He was on his hands and knees again and everything was against him. A trainer came off, a branch hooked his sweater, he banged his head on more thick laurel branches. A strong twig caught the binocular strap and yanked him back and made him think he was being dragged back by the gang. He thought he heard cries and the sound of running. A thorn tore the skin on his forehead and blood trickled into his right eye. When he reached the street lamp he hugged it to stop himself keeling over like a drunken man.

A twig snapped. Then another in the bushes. They were coming. Creeping along. To the astonishment of Spot Sam tottered up the garden path of a house where he could see a family watching television. Sam slumped on their front step ready to ring the doorbell to prevent himself being taken.

Nothing happened. Spot calmly licked the blood from Sam's face then sat on the strange gravel path to await orders. Sam sat on the step and slowly, very slowly felt the use return to his limbs. Then order returned to his mouth—he stopped muttering and whispering. His breathing and pulse returned to a more normal level. Finally his mind became rational again. A little of the guilt strangely returned. After five minutes he returned to the last lamp. Spot wagged his tail and looked up at Sam hoping for another adventure. Clearly there was no one about. What if . . . ? What if John was in some sort of trouble? But no way was he going to look. But he stood and listened. Softly, carried along in the cold frosty air he could just hear the mad laughing-crying sound. And the more he listened the more he was convinced it was a sound of real distress.

He almost returned to help. But as a possibility that did not last long. It suddenly entered his mind that John might have been attacked by one of the dangerous adults children were always being warned against. He wished the irritating sneaking thread of guilt would stop getting into his mind. I am *not* to blame, he shouted to himself in his mind. He decided he would run to the Snow's house. In fact he turned and set off.

In the distance the Snow's house glowed like a halogen beacon. All the security lights were on. He could see the quivering lights of police beacons. The air vibrated with panic even at this distance. Then Sam came to a stop. He could hear Mrs Snow's voice in his mind. 'How strange *you* found him, of all people.' He would get the blame and he could see himself being branded as a bully and a murderer of her chick. And John would lie in his own way to get out of running away. Sam stopped in his tracks. He was trapped. If he told the Snows, they would make remarks, sly suggestions. If he left John, and if John really needed help, then the surprising guilt he felt would grow and grow. What if John were dying?

He thought of an anonymous phone call. But they would know it was a child and in any case John had seen him. His only hope now was to go home and tell everything to his father. At least his mum and dad were not talking to each other. That meant his dad would deal with it. Even though his dad was depressed at the moment he would sort things out. He did not look for hidden motives like his mum had done with the jacket. Sam set off home. He wished he could just go home. But he knew John could not be left. He wished he could but he knew he could not live with the guilt if anything happened to John. He hoped that Mrs Snow would not bully his father and twist everything round. Sighing, Sam trudged homewards.

'Hi, Spuddo!' It was James. He was cheerful from seeing his friends and from two pints of lager. To James's astonishment Sam launched himself at him with such force James nearly fell over. Sam hugged him as he had hugged the lamp-post. Sam had not hugged James like that since he was four.

'I've found John. I don't want anyone to know. I'll get blamed at school and at home. I know I will. But we'll have to go and get him.'

Sam had never really appreciated his oldest brother until that moment. But thinking about it afterwards Sam realized James never did ask boring questions or make unnecessary criticisms. When they had gone on family camping holidays and Sam had wanted to spend all his holiday pocket money on a fishing rod, it was James who had gone with him and bought the rod and fished with him. He made no remarks like his father or mother such as, 'That's all the money you'll have and there'll be none left.' Or, 'You'll be bored with it by dinnertime and no money to buy anything else.'

Once on holiday Sam had wanted to cycle and wanted to hire a bike for a day. James had gone with him. His father said, 'He'll be worn out by ten.' But he and James had cycled along the cliffs for the whole day, a day Sam never forgot. And James said nothing now. He made no comment on Sam's scratched and bleeding face, his filthy jeans and sweater.

'Where is he?'

'On the flats' roof.'

'Come on then.'

The flats had lost their terror. Sam always carried a tiny torch on his key ring. He never used it but he took it out with him simply because he liked it. He shone the tiny beam on the dusty stairs. On the second landing they found a much smaller flight of stairs that led upwards. They could smell fresh air and saw a door open at the top, framing the night sky like a picture in a space book. Sam wondered at the lack of fear in him. Twenty minutes ago he had thought he was going to die from sheer fright.

They found John against the three foot high wall that ran all the way round the flat roof. John had been tied up with some brand new rope and bound securely to the stump of an old communal television aerial. He had been tied so that he was forced to look over the wall with his back to the exit. His brand new army-style camping knife was wedged in the rope. It made John appear as if he had been stabbed in the back. John's trainers had been stolen and there was a scrawled note fastened to the blade. Sam flashed his torch on the paper.

James soon had him untied. As James remarked to Sam later, if John had struggled more he would soon have wriggled free. But John was stricken by a terrible grief. His fantasy of freedom and power and escape was shattered. The very people he admired had turned on him and mocked him. A world of fantasy he had built was in ruins. To Sam's great horror John took hold of James's hand and took Sam's in the other. He had to, he was stiff with cold and shock and cramp. He had been there for almost three hours.

The gang had tied a hanky round John's mouth. This fell off after an hour but by then all John could do was to make a dry hiss like a baby cuckoo and eventually the hoarse hysterical sobbing that Sam had thought was both crying and laughter. Sam wanted to laugh as they went down the stairs. John was in stockinged feet and it was like leading a fat overgrown toddler. And the knife in his back, that had been funny too. Sam bit his lip in the gloom. He wanted to shout out with laughter. Delayed shock and release of tension nearly made him lose control of himself.

John collapsed on the ground outside much as Sam had earlier. James began talking to him as if he were a young child. Sam looked on with amazement as John looked up to him and tried to be as brave as James suggested. Once more Sam felt volcanic laughter about to erupt as John took James's hand again and away he went in his socks.

But panic returned to Sam when they reached the lamp-post and saw the white glare of the Snow's house in the distance. As they approached Sam could see in the distance a policeman standing by the door like Number Ten Downing Street. Mrs Snow wanted police protection against the press and she got it, of course. Sam began to tremble slightly as he thought of what she would make of all this. But he had not taken James into account.

James suddenly yanked John into a clump of trees at a slight bend of the road.

'Look, kid, I don't know who tied you up and dumped you up there. You'll be able to tell the police that, and your mum, of course. Here's the rope you managed to wriggle out of. You've got that, OK? Sam does not want anyone to know he found and rescued you. Got that too? It's his right. It's what you can do in return for his help. Got all that? Now we're going to watch you from here until you reach safety and that big fat policeman at your door. Got it?'

John met James's eye and got it. He had always been able to respect power when he saw it. Even now when his hopes and dreams had fallen apart he could detect James was a better friend than enemy. But he did not reply or thank Sam. Old habits die hard. John staggered down the road with the rope trailing behind like the tail of a defeated jungle animal. They saw him totter in through the gate into the arena of white light, heard the cry of the policeman.

'Run, Spuddo!' hissed James and a big shadow and a medium shadow (shaking now with uncontrollable laughter) and a shadow with four legs faded into the night. When a policeman ran out a minute later there was nothing but street lamps, rustling leaves, and a few watchful stars that dared to challenge the lamps of the Snow's house.

Sam yelled goodnight to his parents from the safety of the stairs. The house was silent except for the drone of the television.

'Wash your face and I'll bring you a drink,' James had ordered.

Sam's father pretended to be asleep. His mother called back brightly to let his father know she did not care if they were not talking—though it was very clear to see she did care. Once upstairs Sam cleaned his teeth, his hand shaking with laughter and not fear. The knife in John's back was like a scene from a silly film. He looked at his face in the mirror and was shocked to see how bad it really was. There was a gash over one eye and his cheek was cut in several places. He removed a tiny thorn from one cut and then washed his face carefully. He suddenly realized he had not washed his face during the time John had bullied him. He put TCP on the cuts and gasped at the stinging. He heard James climbing the stairs with beakers in his hand. He heard Richard's voice.

'Is that drink for me, brother dear?'

Sam heard a forbidden word, then the word 'off' from James who then entered Sam's room with the beakers. Sam followed him in and got into bed which felt wonderfully soft. James drank his coffee and munched a biscuit and Sam drank his drinking chocolate. James was one of the few people Sam knew who could be silent for minutes on end and it did not matter. Other people's silences were either disapproval or boredom or sulks or threats but James's were just companionable.

'Telescope OK?' he said after a while.

'I saw Mercury the other night.' Sam was aware of Richard hovering and nosing out on the landing.

'Right, then. I'm here till next Tuesday.' James got up. 'Then I'm off back to Nottingham. I'll leave you my telephone number. See you.'

Sam slid down the bed, snuggled into his pillow, and fell into a deep and dreamless sleep.

164

SIXTEEN

September passed into October and October passed into dull November and John did not return to Crossroads Primary. In fact he was causing Mrs Snow a good deal of worry. She was a very unhappy mother. Firstly there had been the trouble with the police. John said he had been attacked by older boys. He was emphatic about that. He told his mother, 'I went to the flats to play. I was really fed up with school and Mrs Highfield.' Some boys caught him, he said. But he did not see their faces. When they tied him up he was facing the other way. He was shown photographs by the police but he refused to recognize anyone. There had been a mega tantrum when the police had wanted John to visit the local comprehensive school to try and identify his attackers. He had fallen to the marble floor in the hall and refused to move.

Mrs Snow herself blamed the boy Samuel Wilkinson. She was convinced Sam had been secretly bullying John. She tried to make Mrs Highfield exclude Sam but Mrs Highfield refused. Sam was punished by missing a 'fun' games afternoon. She still felt the trouble in the classroom had been 'a typical spat between Year Six boys'. Mrs Snow found herself blocked by both John and the headteacher.

When John had rolled on the hall marble floor Mrs Snow had heard a policeman say, 'He's bananas, that kid in there.' She had been furious. She called in a most expensive child psychiatrist and a team of experts. One golden October afternoon Mrs Snow and the doctor sat in the sunny lounge. Outside the sun was dimmed by the rising dust from where the flats were being demolished. On the coffee table lay a free paper with the headline LOCAL BUSINESSMAN RAZES YOBBO-INFESTED FLATS TO THE GROUND.

The doctor had been talking to John for several days. He told Mrs Snow John was in great distress. He told Mrs Snow that John was suffering from a mild juvenile depression, grieving over something that he had lost, an idea, an ambition, a hope. But what that was John would not say. He said that John was very behind with his work and well below the average for his age. The doctor suggested intensive help in reading and writing to help John catch up with his school work. This would build up his self esteem.

Mrs Snow did not quite agree. That evening she had tackled John about Sam. John looked at her and refused to speak. His mouth settled into an obstinate line. When she mentioned 'a good boarding school' John walked away. The doctor was recalled. (He charged another fee.) He was emphatic. John was grieving over something. He needed help with his school work. Boarding school would push him over the edge. Still privately convinced that Sam was the cause of the trouble Mrs Snow paid for very expensive home tuition.

One afternoon in November Sam had been sent out to buy some milk from the garage. He was feeling quite pleased with himself. In the spelling test that had so scared John, Sam had come third in the class. Today he had come top. Coming out with the milk he walked into Mrs Snow who was filling up her newest car. She gave Sam a long hard stare. She was utterly convinced Sam had bound and gagged her chick. But she was too good a lawyer to say anything. Sam found he did not much care about her. But for some reason that night he wrote James a long letter, as he sometimes did, telling James everything that had happened at home.

In early December the class had to make John another Get Well Soon card. They had made one straight away when they heard John had been attacked and mugged in the flats. Mrs Highfield had told them John was very upset and needed time at home. Today Mrs Highfield told them John was still upset by it all and was not ready yet to come back. Mrs Snow had told her not to tell the children John was receiving special reading and writing lessons at home.

'John is still recovering,' said Mrs Firth. Sam thought she looked pleased about it. 'Let's all have an A4 sheet and write and draw on it for him. You can all send your own message. Then I'll put them all together and bind them and make him a book of them. Sam can put Get Well Soon on the front in his nice lettering.' Sam did. He also drew a proper picture of a New York cop with a gun pointing straight at John. In the gun smoke he wrote 'Get well soon—or else.'

A few days later Mrs Highfield published a very glossy booklet called *Keeping Children Safe at Crossroads Primary School*. One of the rules in the book was that children must never leave the school building unless everyone knew where they were going. Mrs Snow was sent a glossy edition. The other parents had a black and white photocopy. 'You're shutting the stable door after the horse has bolted,' said Mrs Snow acidly. She would have liked to say John was leaving to attend a good boarding school, but the expensive doctor said it was a bad idea and John sulked for three days whenever it was mentioned.

John did not come back for Christmas. Mrs Firth

produced a musical called *Star Jazz*. 'It's a terribly difficult piano part,' she confided in Mrs Stone. 'But I feel, Jane, I can manage it. I feel I can turn my back on the class and play the piano now the Mo—I mean poor John—is not with us. Someone was telling me in the shops he's had to have special private doctors. Some sort of nervous breakdown. Well, he's caused plenty in his time here!'

Sam had a leading part as a singing space captain. Half-way through he had to shoot Adam with a ray gun and a song because Adam and half the singers, called a Mutant Chorus, had designs on the universe. Sam was a bit friendly with Adam but things were not the same. The rest of the class were very friendly now. But Sam had no special friends.

In January, during a day of slush and fog and cold, Sam's dad heard that John and his mum and dad had gone to Africa for a fantastic holiday together. John had managed to catch up with his work very well and the expensive doctor said the family needed time together, needed time to get to know one another. 'Nice for some,' joked Sam's dad who had called to collect his Job Seekers' money.

Despite the bad weather of January and February spring came early that final year for Sam in the junior school in Year Six. On April the eighteenth the cuckoo returned to the fields and woods that it considered were its own. On that beautiful April day the class were busy preparing their own personal folders of work that was to accompany them to their new comprehensive school. Sunshine filled the classroom and the air hummed with activity and the flip-flop-flap of Mrs Firth's summer classroom sandals that had come out early that year. She suddenly made a dive under a pile of work portfolios and brought out a video. She silenced the class and waved the tape in the air like a trophy.

'Remember this?'

It was the cuckoo video that had been on loan from the museum. The class had missed the final section. Soon after John's adventure the police came into the school and did a project on the dangers of running off alone, so the final part was never shown. Mrs Firth had reordered it.

'We never quite finished this, did we?' She smiled brightly. 'Or the project.' She blew the dust off the pile of cuckoo project folders. 'Some of them were very good. Some of you may wish to take work from them and put it in your sample of work for your new school.'

Later in the afternoon they watched the end of the film. It showed the event-packed journey of the young cuckoo on its way to Africa where it spent the winter. But as late March approached, the cuckoo set off on a journey that would take it back to England. And there the film ended.

'So the cuckoo returns and everything begins all over again,' said Mrs Firth cheerfully.

'Has John been to that place in Africa for his holiday?' Jenny asked suddenly.

'Yes, dear,' smiled Mrs Firth. 'When we get back to the classroom we'll look in the atlas to see where John and the cuckoos go.'

The class sauntered drowsily down the sun-warmed corridor leading back to their class. A strong smell of very costly perfume reached their nostrils. Rich, fruity, flowery perfume mixed with something else. Some of the children wrinkled their noses to distinguish the smells but it was Sam who said, 'I can smell a wet dog.'

Standing in a line at the front of the class waiting their return was Mrs Highfield with a professional smile. Next to her was John, taller, leaner, slightly tanned. Next to John was Mrs Snow, sharp and neat as ever but very far from happy. And between John and Mrs Snow was a very wet dog, steaming a little after a dip in the Snow's lilypond, eyes as bright as stars and very certainly not a designer dog. In fact if you had wished to explain the word mongrel this would have been the dog for the job.

John had a dog. The child psychiatrist had insisted that John had a dog. It had to come from a refuge for abandoned dogs. John must choose an abandoned dog, walk it, feed it, groom it, and care for its welfare. In vain did Mrs Snow coolly protest about disease and genetic problems with mongrel dogs. And in any case a dog 'was quite O.O.T.Q. Absolutely, doctor, out of the question.' But after a stern hour behind closed doors with the doctor she strangely agreed.

Mrs Highfield cleared her throat which always dried out when Mrs Snow flew into the school. She began to speak in her I'm-talking-to-children-so-I'm-talking-very-slowly-and-carefully-because-children-don't-understand voice.

'John is coming back to school today. He has been away for a long time. We are so very glad to welcome you back to Crossroads, John.' This last sentence was for Mrs Snow's benefit. She had made it quite clear that she did not want John back in the school. She would have preferred a good private school. But again she had been overruled by the doctor—and, strangely, John.

The class, who had been fascinated by John in the way a cage of animals might watch the entrance of a dangerous snake, now were fascinated by the dog. The dog was busy round Mrs Highfield's tights where an

170

infant had squirted gravy during Mrs Highfield's dinner patrol. The dog began to lift its leg. John yanked the dog away on its cheap blue nylon lead. (The doctor had insisted on ordinary cheap leads and collars.) The class's interest trebled. Had John changed?

'Welcome back, John,' croaked Mrs Firth. Her throat and jaw muscles had become strangely tense and clenched when she saw John. With a tense movement she moved away some books and papers on Adam's table, the place which John had once called his own.

'Sit down in your place, John, and again, welcome back.' Her voice was cracked, hoarse with horror.

'I'm not sitting there. I'm sitting with Sam. He'll help me with my work. I know he will. He's always been my friend really. We just had a bit of aggro back in September, that's all.'

John gave his mother a defiant glance. A deep silence settled in the room. Mrs Firth's locked jaw relaxed into open amazement. The only sound in the room was a soft, nervous, scrabbling fidgeting from Adam. His pencil case fell to the floor with a soft thud. Then there was the sound of a zip as Jenny put her new birthday pen back in her pencil case, then a rustle as she put the pencil case back in her bag. John advanced towards Sam's empty table.

John's mother stared ferociously with bird of prey eyes. She was absolutely certain Sam had bullied and mugged John. Her courtroom gaze took in John's progress. She was certain John was afraid of Sam. If only, she thought, she had all the evidence, all the facts . . . but John had been too scared to tell the whole story. And yet . . . John looked as happy as he had on his birthday night, that night in September when he had gone off with the boys. Love battled with suspicion in Mrs Snow's brain.

One of John's hands held the dog's lead. The other held a plastic carrier bag from the airport. John rummaged in the bag and brought out two heavy, securely-wrapped magazines. They were expensive astronomy magazines that Sam had never been able to afford. Not that they would have been any good to him because he did not have the hardware they needed. John threw the magazines down on to Sam's table.

'Here. They're for you.'

There was an almost pleading, almost sad look in his eyes. The last time it had been there was in Spain when he joined the other boys playing football on the hilltop—only nobody had been there to see it. But there were plenty of other feelings mixed in his expression. Challenge—and perhaps a little grief.

'You can come and use my web site. You can find out all you want to know about space. We'll sort out the universe together. And you can use the electronic mail to write to your brother, if you like.'

A ripple of disquiet shuddered round the class and their eyes were as round as Mrs Snow's lilypond goldfish's eyes were when the dog jumped in.

Sam made room for John to sit down. This was the new universe, still unmapped, still unknown. He felt oddly calm and without feeling. A flicker of cold fear like cold fire, like the aurora borealis on a frosty night, had flickered and was gone. Perhaps it was the numbness he had felt earlier when John had been bullying him. But now, although he felt little, he did feel able to cope with John.

Sam smiled faintly. Mrs Snow saw it and was suspicious once more. However, Sam was thinking of the knife stuck in John's back, a scene that still made him roll about on his bed with laughter when he was alone. But the knife was only a detail really. It was James who had given him the anchor during that terrible time. There was always James to ring or talk to if anything went wrong.

'You can come walks with me,' John was saying. 'My dad's bought up all the fields and woods round where the flats were. It's yours to explore. We can take the dogs and make a den there now the other one's gone.'

John arranged his things. The large marine boot pencil case frowned upon the whole class from his new seat near the door. He gave the dog a pat on the head.

'OK, Ben. See you, boy. Good dog.' He handed the chewed wet blue-nylon lead to his mother. She took it and left the room and the dog whisked her through the door in an unusually undignified exit. Mrs Highfield followed her, smiling, thinking everything was for the best in the best of schools. The class heard a few murmured words outside the door. Then Mrs Highfield returned. 'Well, that *is* nice. I always knew our anti-bullying policy was a huge success.' She spoke loudly in the hope that Mrs Snow, now being pulled away at high speed, would hear. 'Yes . . . well . . .' Now Mrs Snow had gone she was at a loss for words. Then she saw the cuckoo projects. Relief that all was well made her spout words. 'I think we've all been a lot of very silly cuckoos!'

Nobody laughed. John and Sam arranged their books with infinite care, each careful not to touch the other, as though they were mapping out territory in a new world. Outside, far away in Mr Snow's new woods came the sound of two cuckoos shouting in the April afternoon. Spring and everything else was beginning all over again, as Mrs Firth would say.

Acknowledgements

I would like to thank Mary and Rebecca Green for helping me with the typescript of *Cuckoos*. Without their patient help the book would not exist.

Other Books by Roger J. Green

Daggers
ISBN 0 19 275125 5

'I was responsible for the death of a man once. I know I was. People would say I murdered him. I know I did. I killed him . . . His name was Edward. And I killed him.'

When Caroline reluctantly goes to see her Great-Aunt Clara in the old people's home, she is unprepared for the revelations that follow. Surely her aunt must be rambling; under the influence of all the medicines she is taking for the illnesses that have landed her in the home? How could her boring old aunt, who had spent all her life as a librarian, possibly have killed anyone?

But her aunt's confession seems to help Caroline in her own struggles to come to terms with her feelings for her parents. Maybe the key to her own animosity towards her father lies in the past and the family history her father is so keen to keep secret?

The Throttlepenny Murder

ISBN 0 19 275052 6

Jessie hated old Throttlepenny, her mean-spirited boss. She spent her days dreaming of ways to hurt him, but she'd never have the nerve to turn her dreams into reality.

But Throttlepenny is murdered. It's Jessie that the police come for, and Jessie that winds up in jail. Will someone prove her innocence—before she's hanged?

' . . . a most compelling novel.'

Junior Bookshelf

' . . . a cleverly plotted thriller, misleading the reader in several directions right up to the end.'

The Times Literary Supplement

'The narrative is gripping. There is descriptive writing of a very high quality . . . '

School Librarian

Other Oxford fiction

Chandra

Frances Mary Hendry
ISBN 0 19 275058 5
Winner of the Writer's Guild Award and the Lancashire Book Award

Chandra can't believe her luck. The boy her parents have chosen for her to marry seems to be modern and open-minded. She's sure they will have a wonderful life together. So once they are married she travels out to the desert to live with him and his family—only when she gets there, things are not as she imagined.

Alone in her darkened room she tries to keep her strength and her identity. She is Chandra and she won't let it be forgotten.

Thanis

Hazil Riley
ISBN 0 19 275127 1

'I'm haunted by Thanis. I see her lurking in the shadows. I feel her presence, watching me. I'll never be free of her.'

It is Jessica's big chance, the chance to make her name as an artist. All she has to do is make a silver spiral for the mysterious Thanis? But why is the spiral so important? Does Thanis possess some strange power. Where does she come from? Will Jessica have to pay too high a price for her success?

'Thanis is gripping, mysterious and imaginative, and I couldn't put it down.'
The Bookseller

'Imaginative and well written.'
Junior Times

'I admit I tried to finish Thanis by Hazel Riley while driving— tribute to the great suspense in this . . . story'
The Times

'one of the most original . . . works of fiction I've read for some time. Highly recommended.'
School Librarian Journal

Facing the Dark

Michael Harrison

ISBN 0 19 275053 4

'Everything had changed the moment I opened the door to the two men. It was worse, somehow, that I had been the one to let them in, the one who ended our family life.'

Simon's father has been accused of the murder of a rival cab driver and Simon faces a life branded as the son of a murderer. Then he meets Charley, grieving for her dead father, the murder victim, and they determine to find out the real story behind the murder. Together they can face up to the danger which surrounds them, and bring back some hope for the future.

' . . . the story is well written, fast paced and full of incident'
School Librarian Journal

Shadows

Tim Bowler

ISBN 0 19 275062 3

Jamie's father keeps driving him on to win, to become a world squash champion. But Jamie can't take it any more. He decides to run away with the girl he finds hiding in the shadows, trying to escape from the danger that pursues her.

After a while Jamie realizes he can't run away for ever. He has to come out of the shadows and face up to his father, whatever the cost.

'Tim Bowler scores again with another winning story, *Shadows* . . . A real page turner'
The Bookseller

'Lots of pace, action and a couple of shocking twists!'
The Young Telegraph

'This adventurous tale had me turning pages at a rate of knots. It is exciting and sensational. It is moving and caring.'
Books for Keeps

Sea Dance
Will Gatti

ISBN 0 19 275090 9

Willie Cormack hates the sea. He sees it in his nightmares, the savage ocean full of the ghosts of drowned fishermen, hands reaching out to pull him down into the dark.

Then the tiny community in which he lives is thrown into turmoil by a lone sailor who is suddenly thrust among them. In the atmosphere of bigotry and suspicion that follows, a terrible tragedy seems inevitable unless Willie can overcome his fears. Can he pit himself against the elements that haunt his dreams? Can he face the raging sea?

'Read it for the language. It's very seldom that one comes across a lyrical voice without a trace of soppiness. Gatti knows how to make words work all sorts of magic.'
Times Educational Supplement

'good characterisation and a clear sense of place.'
Daily Telegraph

' . . . there is some excellent writing and Will Gatti is a name I shall look out for in future.'
School Librarian Journal